D0471185

ALSO BY DANIEL SWEREN-BECKER

The Ones

*The Between: An Original Story in the
World of The Ones*

THE
EQUALS

DANIEL SWEREN-BECKER

New York

[Imprint]
MAKE YOUR MARK

A part of Macmillan Publishing Group, LLC
175 Fifth Avenue, New York, NY 10010

Library of Congress Cataloging-in-Publication Data

Names: Sweren-Becker, Daniel, author.
Title: The equals / Daniel Sweren-Becker.
Description: First edition. | New York : Imprint, 2017. | Series: The Ones |
    Summary: Desperate to save her boyfriend, James, from The Equality Team,
    Cody seeks assistance from a radical named Kai, leader of a shadowy rebel
    group, who has a secret, dangerous plan.
Identifiers: LCCN 2016056982 (print) | LCCN 2017027704 (ebook) |
    ISBN 9781250083173 (Ebook) | ISBN 9781250083166 (hardcover)
Subjects: | CYAC: Science fiction. | Adventure and adventurers—Fiction. |
    Genetic engineering—Fiction.
Classification: LCC PZ7.1.S946 (ebook) | LCC PZ7.1.S946 Eq 2017 (print) |
    DDC [Fic]—dc23
LC record available at https://lccn.loc.gov/2016056982

Our books may be purchased in bulk for promotional, educational, or business
    use. Please contact your local bookseller or the Macmillan Corporate and
    Premium Sales Department at (800) 221-7945 ext. 5442 or by e-mail at
    MacmillanSpecialMarkets@macmillan.com.

Book design by Natalie C. Sousa

Imprint logo designed by Amanda Spielman

First edition, 2017

1 3 5 7 9 10 8 6 4 2

fiercereads.com

To any thief that would steal this sequel, suffer a curse without any equal.

THE
EQUALS

PROLOGUE

YOU KNOW INSTANTLY that this will be what kills you. You might have a few minutes left, but nothing more. What will you do with your last moments alive?

You wonder how this even happened. You look over at the mayhem exploding around you, and you realize it was probably inevitable. This is what you signed up for, isn't it? This is what you wanted. In a way, you caused all of this to happen.

And now you have a bullet in your chest to prove it.

The specifics of how this happened no longer seem important. There is the big picture to consider now. Isn't that what these final moments should be about? And in the big picture, you can feel good about dying like this—with honor, with pride, with the knowledge that you fought until your dying breath to protect the Ones.

This fight defined your brief life, but it was meaningful enough to be worth it. You stood up for a group of people who needed help. A group that was vulnerable to the powerful forces of society and the whims of an older, fearful generation. When the government outlawed genetic engineering and then turned the Ones into second-class citizens with the Equality Act, you helped nurture this fight into a movement, a tidal wave that won't end with your death. Dying is a lot easier to accept knowing that you will leave behind a legacy, that your peers will always remember the echo of your name.

Easier, maybe, but still painful. The wound in your chest is making a weird sucking sound, and you know this means a lung has been punctured. The bullet somehow exited your lower back, which means it smashed into a rib bone and ricocheted around your torso like an angry wasp.

Each breath burns now with searing pain, even as a chill descends over your body. *Just a few more minutes*, you ask of your weakening heart. There are just a few more thoughts you'd like to have.

You think about family and what that word means to you now. You think about your mother and the bridge you tried to rebuild. You think about the generation to come and how they might remember you.

You dig your fingers into the cool grass, look up at the perfect bluebird sky, and almost smile. The world will keep spinning without you. The universe will keep humming. And in the blink of a cosmic eye, your body, your country, your planet will swirl away like specks of dust in the wind. It's just that you will be going a moment earlier.

And finally, you think about the person you love.

You suddenly catch sight of this person, moving through the trees, staring back at you. It's too dangerous to get up, not that you'd be able to anyway, so this final look will have to do. You are thankful for the look and thankful for everything you shared. In a life that became over-run with hate and violence and tragedy, at least you also learned about love. It reminded you why the fight was worth it.

You die in amazement at the contradictions that can exist in this world. Awestruck by what our species has accomplished and also what we are willing to do to each other. Societies built on miracles of human ingenuity and societies destroyed just the same. It is hard to fathom, yet you watched it happen in your own short lifetime. But with your last breath, your final thought is about an even greater contradiction. Something that is harder to swallow, yet still undoubtedly true. Something, ironically, that you wouldn't be able to live with even if you survived. It is about the person looking back at you through the trees.

You love this person. This person betrayed you.

CHAPTER 1

Three weeks earlier

CODY COULD BARELY breathe. It had nothing to do with the thick cloud of ash that descended on her or the grueling trek through the woods. No, the vise grip on her chest was entirely about James.

As she ran free, he was in chains. And even worse, she ran free *because* he was in chains. He had come back for her. Saved her. Sacrificed himself for her. His reward for all that was being apprehended by his own brother and an Equality Team, shipped off to an internment camp, and subjected to the Vaccine—the government's brutal attempt to somehow undo the genetic engineering bestowed upon the Ones.

Cody had watched James's capture from across the river, helpless to intervene. Now she knew that if by some miracle she ever saw him again, he would be a totally different person. Almost too distracted to run, Cody gasped for air, desperate for it not to be true.

"Come on, Cody, keep moving!" came a yell from up ahead.

Kai stretched back his arm and yanked her over a fallen tree, while Taryn pushed branches out of the way. It was just the three of them now, and Cody was struck by how calm Kai looked. Apparently she was the only one still traumatized by what had happened at the river's edge. It had only been a few minutes, but Kai was already in planning mode.

It was a small relief for Cody to be trailing after him. Kai was the unofficial leader of the New Weathermen, the group fighting back against the government on behalf of the Ones. Although their battle that morning had ended in defeat at the Shasta quarry, she was confident Kai had a contingency plan.

"Where are we going?" she asked.

Kai exchanged a look with Taryn, who seemed equally calm about the whole situation. Cody had to admit that a part of her resented their easy nonchalance. A forest fire was raging behind them, on the far side of the valley they had just crossed. All the other Ones who fought with them had been captured and were on their way to internment camps. From Cody's perspective it seemed pretty bleak. They had nowhere to go, no one to help them.

"We can camp in the woods tonight," Kai said. "But the

Equality Teams will still be looking for us tomorrow. We're going to have to disappear."

Disappearing was going to be difficult. There was a federal order for all the Ones to be rounded up, and a travel party with their looks was sure to stick out. Still, Kai and Taryn pressed ahead, into the unknown. Cody followed, but already, in her own mind, a different plan was starting to take shape.

"And what about James?" she said.

"What about him?" Taryn asked. "You saw what happened. Now you need to forget about him."

So much for the brilliant contingency plan, Cody thought. But Taryn's suggestion wasn't going to work, either. Cody knew that forgetting about James was impossible.

She had a promise to keep.

≈

Later that day, after they had put enough distance between themselves and the fire, Cody, Kai, and Taryn stopped at a dry creek bed. A muddy rock overhang provided some shelter, and they collapsed against the angled wall, unlaced their boots, and tossed aside the guns they had been carrying from the quarry. Even in their exhaustion, they were mesmerized by the sight above them; as the sun dipped below the horizon in the distance, the smoldering forest painted the sky with psychedelic reds and oranges.

Cody remembered the beautiful dawn of this same day and couldn't believe everything that had happened since.

The New Weathermen had made their stand at the quarry to resist the Equality Team. Cody—suddenly a runaway, a fugitive, an accomplice in the death of her boyfriend's father—had determined she was prepared to die for this cause, and she took up arms against her own government. Somehow, amid all that chaos, she experienced a moment with Kai that was loaded with feelings she was afraid to acknowledge. And he had revealed something to her also—secrets that no one was supposed to know. Again, she was almost too scared to understand him fully. She hadn't even bothered to try at the time, knowing that she was about to die.

And she no doubt would have died, if not for James. He set the fire and led them out of it, then made sure they got away safely. James's actions had provoked an even more powerful feeling, one that she wasn't afraid to name. It was true love. A feeling of desperate attraction, awestruck admiration, and perfect understanding. And then, just minutes after she felt it, her chance to share it was torn away. James had fought to make that brief moment possible. Now it was her turn to get it back.

"We need to save James. I don't care how hard it is," she said.

Kai looked over at her, almost irritated. "Cody, we have to be smart," he said. "Obviously we want to get all the Ones out of the camps. But we can't just run straight after James. We have to think bigger."

"We can't waste any time," Cody said. "They're going to give him the Vaccine. I'm going to save him with or without you two."

Cody stared at Kai and Taryn. They looked exhausted, filthy, and defeated. She was reminded that they were only nineteen, a few years older than her. And she knew their dreams of a successful rebellion had taken a powerful hit that morning.

Kai had promised they would win the day or become echoes—everlasting reminders of the fight for freedom. But somehow neither of those results had come to pass. They were just tired and dirty and stuck in the woods. Cody could hardly believe it.

She stood up. "Seriously—I am going after James." She waited, but no one moved. "You're really just going to lie here? Kai? Is this how you planned to end 'the loudest day of our lives'?"

Kai wouldn't meet Cody's eyes. But Taryn glared at her.

"You heard him," Taryn said. "We can't risk it right now. A lot of people got taken today. A lot of our friends. So how 'bout you sit down and quit whining about it."

Kai touched Taryn on the arm. "It's fine. Let her go if she needs to." He turned to Cody. "I'll understand if you go alone, and I won't stop you. It's stupid and it's reckless, but I'll understand."

"Wow," Cody said. "So you're just a phony with a cool motorcycle and a nice speech?" Disgusted, she started to gather her things. "Good luck with the rest of your revolution."

Cody could see that Kai wanted to respond, but he swallowed it. There was that ice-cold self-control again. Kai's emotions were his and his alone to reveal.

She stood up and looked out from under their embankment. Night had descended upon the pine trees, but a bright moon filtered through. Cody didn't know exactly where to start, but she knew that she couldn't help James from here. James had saved her all on his own, and he was a choirboy, allergic to trouble. She didn't need Kai and Taryn. She'd do it herself.

But as Cody stepped away from their meager campsite, she heard a shotgun cock behind her. She turned around to find Taryn pointing the gun up at her.

Cody froze, surprised and confused. Kai tried to reach out and gently take the gun from Taryn. But Taryn rose to her feet, stepped forward, and kept it leveled at Cody.

"You're not going anywhere."

"Taryn. Put the gun down, okay?" Kai said softly. Cody looked at him, pleading with her eyes for him to intervene. "Just let her go," he said.

"Believe me, I'd love to. But I can't," Taryn said.

With her heart racing, Cody finally had the nerve to lash out at Taryn. "What's your problem? I mean besides the sullen attitude, the fake toughness, the practiced condescension—what's your problem with *me*?"

Cody had a guess. It was probably the way that Kai looked at her that pissed Taryn off so much. Now she wondered if Taryn would actually cop to it.

Taryn just laughed, though. "Let's start with the fact that you're a liar. That you're not even a One. And then add that you need to be rescued every two minutes like some helpless puppy dog. First you get caught by the cops at the school takeover. Then you run into the blast zone when we bomb the vaccine lab. And today you get us stuck in a forest fire. I'm tired of having to look out for your utterly normal, non-genetically-engineered ass."

Cody's anger made her forget that she was staring at the wrong end of a shotgun. "I didn't get us stuck in that fire; James did. And you'd be dead if it wasn't for him. That's the person I am going to save. So how about you let me leave? Wouldn't that make you happy?"

"I'd throw a freaking parade," Taryn said, then paused. "But unfortunately for all of us, I heard what Kai told you."

Instantly, Cody could see that this changed everything. And Kai grimaced, too—it was clear that he knew Taryn was right.

Taryn turned to him. "You shouldn't have told her that stuff."

"I thought we were about to get killed," Kai said. "She deserved to know."

Cody knew what this was about now. It was about Edith Vale and the Ark.

That morning, Kai had started to tell her a secret that didn't make any sense. Prior to that, Cody had only known that Edith Vale was the government agent who had released the list of Ones, exposing them all to targeted persecution. And the theoretical, gigantic, secret Ark was the reason why Agent Norton had tortured Cody so ruthlessly. Edith Vale and the Ark shouldn't have anything to do with each other.

But Kai had implied something different. He said Edith Vale was at the Ark right now. He said Cody would have enjoyed meeting her.

So the Ark was an actual place. Edith Vale was with the Ones, on their side. And now Taryn was pissed that Cody knew.

"We can't risk her blowing our cover," Taryn said.

"I would never do that," Cody responded.

"Maybe not intentionally. But what if you get captured?" Taryn asked. "Again," she added sourly.

"I already proved I could handle that. They did everything they could to me when I was captured the first time, and I didn't say a word."

Kai stared at her, unmoved, and Cody felt her stomach sink. "Yeah. But that was before you actually knew something. You didn't have anything to reveal," he said. "Taryn's right. I'm sorry, Cody, it's too risky to let you leave by yourself. We have to stay together, the three of us."

"Wow. What a great silver lining," Taryn grumbled

sarcastically. But to Cody's relief, at least she lowered the gun.

"I still need to save James. If you're not going to help me, you can either shoot me now or tie me up, but I'm going to sneak off the first chance I get."

Taryn looked at Kai and shook her head. For all their arguing, they were in the same place where they'd started. But Cody saw Kai start to nod, as if he was finally accepting an outcome that was inevitable the whole time.

"There's only one person who can help you save James now," he said, looking Cody square in the eyes. "So let's go to the Ark and meet Edith."

CHAPTER 2

KAI WOKE UP before dawn, as the birds in the trees above them began to squawk in the darkness. He was pissed that both Cody and Taryn were still sleeping. There was a lot to do that day, and they had to get moving. There was a lot to do every day, Kai knew by now. Fighting the entrenched majority for freedom wasn't easy, and Kai had come to accept that he was going to shoulder a disproportionate share of that burden. He didn't resent this duty, though. In fact, he was damn proud of it.

He knew the rest of the Ones needed people like him, people on the front lines who were devoting their lives to this cause. Kai didn't begrudge some of the Ones for being too scared or too young to throw themselves into the fight. They would need to step up eventually, of course.

But it was his job to lead the way, to spark that fire, and he was confident they would rise to the occasion.

Kai took his responsibility literally for the moment and got to work poking at the dying embers of their campfire. Small flames kicked back to life, and Kai debated waking up the girls. *Maybe it's better to let them rest now*, he thought, considering the trek ahead of them. He sat back against the overhang and found himself staring at Cody as she slept, the first light from the sun bouncing warmly off her cheeks.

It was hard to sort out exactly what had happened just a day earlier. So much had gone wrong in their fight against the Equality Team, but Kai's thoughts kept drifting back to that moment with Cody on the ridge. Both of them were certain they were about to die, so they locked hands and shared something. But that moment was impossible for him to understand now, the tenderness so foreign to him, and so unlikely for Cody, that he didn't trust his memory. It was a confusing blur, and most of all, it was a distraction.

Figuring out that moment with Cody wasn't going to help the Ones. And that's all that Kai cared about.

It was a small miracle that Kai was even able to sit around considering this problem. He had woken up the day before prepared to die for this cause, and it had looked like he would do exactly that. The Weathermen at the quarry were surrounded and outgunned. Kai sure as hell would have never let himself be taken away to one of the internment camps, so his death seemed only minutes away. He remembered making his peace with that.

It hadn't exactly been a shock to prepare to die like that. Kai never pictured himself making it to retirement age, kicking back on a rocking chair, playing with his grandchildren. Those were working-stiff aspirations that had never appealed to him. Maybe he had the genetics for a long life, but he definitely didn't have the disposition. So a violent death at nineteen was something Kai considered a job hazard. The fight to protect the Ones was his life's work, and he knew the most likely way it would end.

Kai hadn't figured on James, though. It pissed him off to admit, but James had saved all of them, and in spectacular fashion, no less. He had come out of nowhere to pull off a hell of a move, and it threw Kai for a loop. He had started that day resolved to end up as either a hero or a martyr, yet somehow he was neither. Instead, he was just humbled and indebted to James.

More important, though, he had been given a reprieve. Kai tried to fix his mind only on this: He now had a second chance to accomplish his goals. He wasn't used to getting favors or handouts, so he might as well take advantage of this one. As he sat alone staring into the fire, Kai resolved to keep up the fight and aim higher. First, he would need to make it safely to the Ark and reunite with Edith Vale.

They would expand their fight against the government's far-reaching Equality Act. Protect all the Ones who couldn't fight for themselves. Save their peers from the Vaccine. And most enjoyably, strike back at the lunatics in the Equality Movement. Kai began to relish this unlikely opportunity. He would grab it by the throat and accomplish something greater. With this second chance he would live on in the echoes of history, after all.

Newly energized, Kai stood up and brushed the twigs off his clothes. He stepped out from the embankment and walked downhill to a thin stream trickling through the creek bed, where he knelt and cupped some water into his mouth. Spending an afternoon racing away from a forest fire had left him ravenous and dehydrated.

"Save some for me, please."

Kai lifted his head and saw Cody walking up behind him. She was rubbing the sleep from her eyes and stretching her back like a cat. Not for the first time, Kai marveled at the fact that Cody wasn't actually a One. It was still hard to believe someone could look like that without the help of a very talented genetic engineer. As she got closer, Kai finally remembered to stop staring.

"Permission for the prisoner to take a drink?" Cody asked.

"Cody, you're not a prisoner."

"Right. I'm just not allowed to leave."

"We're all going to the Ark. Edith is going to want to

liberate James and everyone else just as much as you do. She's going to help us."

"Edith Vale released the List. She changed my life. And she put a target on the back of every One in the country. Why would she help us?"

"She's not who you think she is. Trust me."

"How about you trust me? If you're going to hold me hostage over this information, the least you could do is actually tell me the truth," Cody said sternly.

Kai had learned by now that sharing information just made things worse for everyone. When he had hinted about this stuff on the ridge yesterday, he didn't think it mattered anymore. Now he clearly saw that the less Cody knew, the easier it would be to proceed without everyone fighting.

"Edith isn't an enemy. She's on our side. You'll understand once we get to the Ark." And then Kai couldn't resist pushing Cody's buttons. "And besides, prisoners don't need to be looped in on the plans."

Cody shook her head and tried not to smile. "I'm serious," she said. "Have you met her before?"

"Yes."

"How long have you known her?"

"She reached out a couple years ago, when the New Weathermen were just getting started. Before the List, obviously."

"And why do you trust her?" Cody asked pointedly.

Kai stared at her. "Because she's exactly like you." He meant it, but, more important, Kai also knew that would shut her up.

Cody appeared a bit taken aback, but was apparently satisfied for now. She turned and walked back toward their camp. Again, Kai held his gaze on her. He had determined to make his second chance about fighting for the Ones, but he knew there were other reasons to celebrate being alive. Keeping that all straight was the hard part.

=

They trudged through the woods back toward civilization and eventually found a quiet country road. Kai pointed them south, keeping them at the edge of the forest, out of sight. He knew that the roundup of all the Ones was still in progress. They'd been ordered by the federal government to report to internment camps—and any Ones who didn't comply were being forced into the camps against their will. Which meant Equality agents were bound to be everywhere, and a trio of fit, good-looking teenagers were sure to draw attention.

For two days, they stayed concealed during the day and moved quickly at night. Once, Kai risked going into a run-down country store to buy food. The bored clerk barely even looked at him as Kai scooped up an obscene amount of jerky, nuts, and water.

Finally, with their feet aching, Kai knew they were close. Not to the Ark—that was tucked away high up in the Cascade Mountains—but to a rail yard outside of Sacramento. That's where they were going to hitch their ride.

Once they arrived at the perimeter of the Union Pacific rail yard, Kai led them around to the northern edge, to where they wouldn't have to climb a fence. The trains heading north emerged slowly from the yard into flat, dusty fields. After the sun went down, it was the perfect catch-out, a free ride across the rocky scrubland and eventually into the mountains of the Pacific Northwest.

As they looked down at the trains, waiting for darkness, hoods pulled up against the wind, Taryn turned to Cody.

"You've rail-hopped before, right?" she asked.

Cody, uncomfortable, didn't respond. Taryn shook her head angrily at Kai. "Don't worry, Cody," Kai said. "It'll be no problem for you. Easy as riding a bike."

"Yeah, if a bike could knock your head clean off when you slip on the pedals," Taryn said. "Seen it before."

"Got it," Cody said. "Then I hope no one slips."

They sat down and watched the trains in silence until it was dark enough to sneak down, then started walking to the rails. Kai wasn't worried about Cody; she had risen to greater challenges than jumping on a meandering train car. He was more concerned that Taryn was going to do something reckless. Maybe it'd be best if they quarantined her in a separate compartment.

A train edged out of the yard and started chugging

along. Kai pointed to the chain of open-sided boxcars in the middle, and they all stepped closer to the track.

"Let's go," he said. "We need to run alongside it."

The train's engine car whirred past, and they started to run. At first the train pushed past them, but they soon matched its speed. The boxcars came into view. Kai let the first one pass. Then, in one fluid motion, he grabbed the lowest rung of an iron ladder, leaped into the air, and swung himself into the dusty car.

Kai turned quickly to look down at Cody, still jogging alongside. "Just like that," he yelled over the clanging metal wheels.

Cody kept pace with the train and grabbed the ladder. She jumped awkwardly and tried to swing herself in, but only her upper body made it. For a second her legs flopped wildly outside the boxcar, dangling just over the rail. She looked up desperately at Kai.

"Kai!"

He was already reaching for her, leaning out of the train and grabbing hold of her jacket to yank her inside. Cody scurried across the floor, away from the opening. A moment later, Taryn popped in easily. She shuffled to the back wall and sprawled out on a tarp.

"All aboard?" Kai asked.

Cody, dusting herself off, nodded. They had all made it in one piece.

Kai went back to the open edge of the boxcar. He felt

the train pick up speed. The clanging underneath built to a perfect percussive rhythm. The shrubby desert outside raced backward into black shadows. And Kai just couldn't resist—he grabbed the ladder, swung his entire body into the darkness, and howled into the wind at the top of his lungs.

=

Out of habit, Kai made sure he was the last one to fall asleep. Taryn was conked out on the tarp, Cody had nestled into a corner, and Kai finally allowed himself to shut his eyes. The train was loud, but its rhythm was soothing. And most of all, for Kai, it was familiar.

He had spent countless hours in train cars like this one. Crisscrossing the country, running scared for some of it, running wild for the rest. That was the life of an orphan who no one wanted.

Kai could barely trust his earliest memories, but he knew the basics. Dead mother. Disinterested father. And then one institution or foster family after another. Each new family always intrigued because he was a One—Kai was forever the shiniest trinket in the orphanage. Of course it never worked out like the adoptive parents thought. Sure, Kai looked like a perfect child, but he was impossible to handle—out of control behaviorally and impossible to reach emotionally.

When these ill-equipped families inevitably sent him back to the state agencies, the feedback loop would only speed up: Kai would grow angrier; someone new would take a chance on him; he'd be even quicker to reveal that he wasn't worth the trouble. And back he'd go. Ditched again. Story of his life.

When he was thirteen, a nice woman named Christine took him in. Things weren't so bad, Kai remembered. Christine understood he needed time to trust her. She didn't force things. Of course Kai never said it out loud, but he started to imagine sticking around this time.

"I've got your back," Christine would always tell him.

Kai knew that normal parents and children said "I love you." But Kai didn't need that. He had given up on finding it. "I've got your back" was enough. It suited him. And Christine kept her promise. After every fight or problem at school, she took his side.

Which is why Kai didn't regret tossing her punk-ass boyfriend down a flight of stairs.

Vince deserved it. He was mean to begin with, and after three drinks he was a terror. He'd toss Christine around their house. Blame her for his miserable life. Scream at her. More and more often, the rants would circle back to the Equality Movement, which was just gaining steam at the time. Its followers longed for a familiar era that didn't exist anymore—an era when all the unwritten rules of society benefited them. Vince believed every word of the propaganda, and he was certain that Ones were ruining the country. During his rants, he'd start eyeballing Kai, the "genny" that Christine had brought into her home. Christine would stand up for Kai, but that just made Vince angrier. One night he had her pinned against the wall, forearm against her throat, choking her, and Kai knew he had no choice.

He was fourteen then, his body almost done transforming into a man. The genetic engineers had set him on a journey toward a perfect physical specimen, and the fruits of their labor were ripening. Kai rushed over and pulled Vince off his foster mom like a rag doll. Vince started swinging at him, but Kai hardly felt it. He had the older, larger man by the collar, and he pushed him forward, crossing the kitchen, ignoring the blows raining down on him, rage building.

And then Kai tossed him against the door to the basement. The door swung open and Vince bounced down the staircase and landed limply on the concrete floor. Kai stood in the doorway and looked at the body below. Vince was sprawled on his chest, but the blank eyes on his twisted head stared straight back up at Kai.

As quickly as Kai knew he was dead, he also knew he had done the right thing. He had to protect Christine. He needed to have her back. And that's why what happened next was so devastating. It was the moment that haunted Kai every day of the four years he spent in a juvenile detention center. And it was the moment when he learned for the final time that growing close to someone could only lead to betrayal.

He looked across the kitchen and saw Christine. Instead of being relieved, she was terrified. And she was dialing 9-1-1.

=

Kai woke with a start when he felt the train slow to a halt. Immediately he knew they shouldn't be stopping. He crawled to the opening of the boxcar and stuck his head out. It was obvious they were at some kind of checkpoint, maybe on the border of California and Oregon. Kai had never seen something like this in his previous experiences on the rails, but he kicked himself for not considering it. The roundup of Ones was still going on, and security everywhere was heightened. The floodlights and bouncing flashlight beams ahead of him confirmed this.

After he ducked back into the train, Kai nudged Cody and Taryn awake.

"Stay quiet," he whispered. "We're at a checkpoint." Kai pointed to the darkest corner of the boxcar and gestured for them to move into the shadows. Then he peeked outside one more time. A guard with a flashlight was walking down the line.

As Kai pressed against the wall, Cody grabbed his arm. "What if they find us?" she asked, barely audible.

Kai shook his head, unsure. He certainly didn't plan to

get taken down by some two-bit security guard on the graveyard shift. But he could hear the man's boots crunching on the gravel, getting closer and closer.

Taryn clicked her tongue and got his attention. With her foot, she pushed back the edge of the tarp she'd been sleeping on. There was a crowbar underneath. Kai nodded. Taryn picked it up and tossed it across the car to him. He caught it silently and edged up to the door.

The guard was close to their car now. Kai could see him stopping at each compartment, shining his light inside and inspecting them, but only very briefly. Maybe he'd see them and maybe he wouldn't. But Kai knew what he would have to do if the guard discovered them. He tried to build up the rage that he would need, the violent, singular energy that would allow him to kill this person. He thought of Vince.

There it was. That familiar adrenaline spike. Kai knew he would do what he had to.

He raised the crowbar above his head as the guard stopped at the edge of their car. The beam of light flitted around inside. Somehow it missed Cody and Taryn's corner. But the guard kept looking in. Kai tightened his grip, his body taut as a spring.

And then the guard kept walking. He was just a lazy, regular guy, who probably wanted to go home. That attitude had just saved his life.

Kai let out a slow, relieved sigh. He placed the crowbar

back on the floor and lowered himself to sit across from Cody and Taryn. There was no chance of sleeping anymore, he knew, not after gearing himself up like that.

Cody looked over at him. "Are we there yet?" she asked, trying to lighten the mood.

"Almost," Kai responded. "Almost."

=

A few hours later, after they had jumped off the train during its long uphill climb into the Cascades, Kai led them deep into the woods. It was a crystal-clear morning, and he was navigating toward the Ark using a distant peak as a landmark. They stopped to rest frequently, out of breath in the thin mountain air. But Kai kept pressing onward, his excitement building.

They were almost at the Ark.

Kai had been there only once before, a year earlier. The Ark was in the process of being built then; it was just a few wooden structures at the bottom of a glen. Edith was obsessed with the construction plans, and she oversaw every beam being put in place. They had felled trees for timber and scavenged everything they needed from the forest. There were only about a dozen Ones working on it, so progress was slow. But Kai knew that the Ark would be finished now, and he couldn't wait to see it.

The Ark was conceived by Edith as a refuge for the Ones—and more specifically now, the New Weathermen. It was a secure, undetectable home base where they could convene and plan their operations. And although no one ever said it outright, it was also designed as a safe haven of last resort. If the rest of the country got too dangerous for them, the Ones could come here. It was almost impossible to find from the outside world, nestled in a remote valley and shrouded from above by towering pines.

As Kai thought about seeing Edith again, he was surprised to feel a pit in his stomach. She was a hero to him, the mastermind behind the Ones' resistance movement. And she was a hard woman to impress. Even as Kai took a leadership role within the Weathermen, he couldn't remember a single moment of praise from Edith. And now he was rolling up to the Ark with Cody, who wasn't even a One. Kai was ready to do more, and he wanted Edith to see that. He'd successfully planned the bombing of the vaccine lab. He'd led a face-off and avoided capture by the Equality Teams. He hoped Edith had taken notice.

Kai was also dying to hear what Edith had been planning. She'd been cryptic with him a year earlier about how they were going to win this fight—how they would finally defeat the Equality Movement. But she made clear she had an ace up her sleeve. It was too early to talk about it, she said. But she assured him the Ones would never be destroyed.

Kai could feel how close they were now. He pointed Cody and Taryn down the slope of a valley, and they slid through the last wall of trees. At last, he saw the buildings up ahead, more of them now, improvements everywhere. And then he saw a figure in a white lab coat step outside.

Edith Vale walked out to greet them. As she took in the traveling party approaching her, Kai saw she didn't look very pleased.

CHAPTER 3

CODY STOOD FROZEN as the woman in the white coat extended her hand.

"Hello. I'm Edith Vale."

After an awkward hesitation, Cody managed to reach out and shake hands. She still couldn't believe she was meeting the woman who had turned her life upside down. If not for Edith Vale and her reckless release of the List, the world would be a lot safer. Everyone wouldn't have gotten a thorough report on the name and location of every single One, right in their in-box. But without the List, Cody also wouldn't have known the truth about herself, how her mother, with the best of intentions, misled Cody, telling her she'd been genetically engineered, that she was a One—even though she wasn't. So as much as she wanted to punch the tall, fit, forty-year-old woman in front of her, Cody also knew that she owed Edith a debt of gratitude and forced herself to stay calm.

"I'm Cody. It's nice to meet you," she said, holding Edith's gaze.

Then Edith turned to Kai and Taryn. "I'm glad you both made it back. I know it's not easy out there right now."

"We found a way," Kai said. He nodded toward Cody. "She deserves a lot of the credit."

Edith looked at Cody. "Hmm. Good to know."

"What the hell did *she* do?" Taryn blurted out. "Am I forgetting something?"

Kai started to respond, but Cody jumped in ahead of him. "Taryn's right. I didn't do anything; it was all James." Cody met Edith's eyes again. "My boyfriend saved us. He's a One, and he's in an internment camp right now. I need you to help me rescue him."

"We hope to save all the Ones stuck in the camps," Edith replied.

"I need to save James *now*. Before he gets the Vaccine. Kai said you would help me."

Edith shot him a look, leading Kai to lower his eyes deferentially. "I just meant that you'd have the best idea about what to do," Kai said. "I didn't mean to suggest that—"

"It's fine, Kai," Edith said, her tone curt. "It's good you're all here."

Cody couldn't believe Kai's behavior. She had never

seen him scared before, never seen him defer to someone else. His body language reminded her of a family dog after being caught neck-deep in a bag of cookies. Cody had always considered him the leader of the New Weathermen, and his confidence was like nothing she'd ever encountered. It was why Cody shivered when he whispered in her ear and tensed up when she felt his eyes on her. But everyone had a boss, it seemed.

Except, Cody suspected, Edith Vale.

"There's a lot to talk about," Edith said. "A lot of plans to make. But you just trekked across a mountain range. Let's get you settled in, and we can figure everything out later."

Cody started to open her mouth, ready to insist they focus on saving James, but Edith put a firm hand on Cody's shoulder. "Welcome to the Ark," she said. "Now let me show you around."

Even as she judged Kai for cowering, Cody somehow felt compelled to listen to this woman. Maybe it was the firm grip on her arm or the look in Edith's eye. As Edith started walking toward the group of wooden buildings arranged in a haphazard semicircle, Cody decided, for the time being, to follow.

Rapid-fire, Edith began explaining each structure. "Mess hall, bunkhouses, generator, tech lab, greenhouse, food storage, armory, forge. That's my little cabin back there. And the big structure behind it, we call it the barn;

it's going to be our research facility. If we ever have time to get it together."

Each building looked to Cody like a log cabin designed by an ambitious architecture student. Made entirely of wood, the structures blended into the surroundings but were clearly constructed with precise tools and measurements. They were all small and modest, with standard doors and windows—except for the research building behind Edith's quarters. Cody could see, even from a distance, its solid steel door, complicated lock, windowless walls, and the vent system on its roof. She wanted to see more, but Edith kept walking.

They passed a few other Ones who nodded at Edith and eyed Cody suspiciously. Most of them seemed a little older than Cody, closer to Kai's age. There was clearly a high-functioning community already in place at the Ark, and Cody was increasingly aware that, not being a One, she might upset its balance.

"You can see it's a nice little spot we've carved out for ourselves here," Edith said as she stopped outside one of the bunkhouses. "Has Kai explained why we built this place?"

Cody shook her head.

"First and foremost, this is a refuge, somewhere off the map where we can always be safe. Who knows how long we'll need to stay here, but I happen to think it could be quite a while. It could be forever. It all depends on the behavior of this planet's most destructive force—a large group of human beings. The predictability of their self-interest eclipsed only by the unpredictability of their stupidity. But no matter how that plays out, I promise you, we'll be ready."

Cody was now more confused than ever about what Edith Vale was trying to accomplish. First she released the List, which threatened all the Ones. Then Kai assured her that Edith was some mastermind who would help their fight against the Equality Movement. And now she was talking about the Ark like an idyllic resort that she never planned to leave. Cody couldn't figure out if this woman was a revolutionary or a cult leader.

As Edith gestured for Cody to enter the bunkhouse, Cody couldn't bite her tongue any longer.

"Why'd you release the List?"

Edith smiled at Cody but didn't answer right away.

"I don't get it," Cody continued. "Do you want to help the Ones or not?"

Edith waited a moment, then finally spoke. "I know who you are, Cody. I know your story, and I know what you went through when you were detained. I know why you endured that, even after you found out the truth about yourself. If you're as smart as I think you are, then you also know why I released the List."

Even as she remained totally clueless, Cody felt a wave of pride crest over her. Edith Vale knew who she was, respected her, knew what she'd been through. It was easy to see why Edith had such sway over her followers. But Cody, still wary, reminded herself not to be seduced so easily.

"Rest up for a bit and find me at dinner later," Edith said. "I'll tell you a pretty crazy story."

=

That afternoon, Cody lay awake on her thin cot, staring up at the spiderwebs on the ceiling. She could hear Kai and Taryn snoring softly on their beds behind her. Even though she was bone-tired, Cody's mind was racing, and sleep wasn't coming. The mystery of Edith Vale consumed her, and her concern for James hadn't diminished, but she realized there was something even more urgent than that: She was starving.

It was nice that dinner had been offered, but Cody was accustomed to eating like five times a day. And that was under normal circumstances, without leaping aboard cross-country trains and climbing up the Cascades. Cody was so ravenous now, she abandoned any hope of getting rest. She sat up, put her shoes on, and tiptoed out of the bunkhouse. Maybe the Ark had a snack bar. If it was truly a refuge for the healthiest teenagers in the country, it better.

As she wandered through the unfamiliar wooded footpaths, Cody contemplated how much her life had changed. This was technically a school day, after all, but the routine of classes, homework, and soccer practice was gone. She couldn't just pop in for a bite at her favorite diner. Even crazier, she couldn't see her mom.

Cody felt a pang of guilt. She hoped her mom wasn't worrying, but that was absurd. Since Cody had taken off, she'd almost died several times. That type of track record kind of justified her mom's concern. At the very least, Cody hoped her mom understood why she had to leave and why she had to commit to this fight. That's what Cody had hoped to convey in the note she had left—that her mom had raised her to be proud of who she was, and even if her superficial identity had changed, her moral compass had stayed intact. A small group of young people were being persecuted unfairly for how they were born. They were Ones and Cody wasn't. It didn't matter. Cody was going to stand by them.

The sun had disappeared behind a mountain, and a cool wind had risen in its absence. Cody realized she had circled around the entire compound and she hadn't even sniffed a vending machine. She looked up to find herself in front of Edith Vale's cabin. A little embarrassed to be caught walking around aimlessly, she hustled away quickly.

Her scamper led to the front of the research building, what Edith had called the barn. And at the moment Cody passed by, she saw the thick steel door start to open. Caught off guard, Cody jumped behind a tree to conceal herself.

This was silly, Cody knew, but she felt like a cat burglar caught with one foot dangling out the window. She didn't know all the rules of this place, and she sensed that sneaking around the entrance to this building would be frowned upon. So now she was stuck with her body pressed to the bark, hoping no one would discover her.

As Cody waited, she heard the door close and the heavy-duty lock engage. It was only a few feet away from her, and surely whoever was leaving the building would be walking right past her in a second.

Cody held her breath and tried to shrink into herself. She pinned her hopes on rotating around the tree in perfect unison with the person walking by, a maneuver she had to admit was cribbed straight from Looney Tunes.

Unfortunately, the trunk of the tree wasn't very thick. Cody could tell from the sound of the footsteps pausing that she'd been discovered.

"Hello?" she heard.

Cody peeked out from behind the tree to find a dazzling young woman who immediately smiled at her.

"Hi there."

Cody tried to cover her embarrassment. "Hi. I was just stretching my legs and got a little lost."

"It's beautiful out here, isn't it?"

"Yeah. And a little quieter than I'm used to," Cody said.

"So you're new, I take it. I'm Ramona."

Cody reached out to shake Ramona's hand. "Cody. I just got here today. With Kai and Taryn."

"Oh, I'm so glad they're back. That they're safe, I mean. And it's good to see that they brought reinforcements. The more the merrier up here," Ramona said.

Cody was having trouble following along—that's how strikingly beautiful this girl was. But more than her beauty, Cody was struck by the warmth of her energy— the sincerity of her smile and the kindness of her gaze. The only thought Cody could formulate was how desperately she wished Ramona was her big sister. With her few functioning brain cells, Cody still realized that would be a weird thing to blurt out. So she tried to compose herself.

"I didn't mean to sneak up on you, I swear," Cody said.

"Don't worry about it. I've been here for more than a year, and I still remember what it was like my first few days. It feels like some kind of top-secret fortress, right?"

Cody couldn't believe that some of the Ones had been here for that long. It made her even more curious about the research building Ramona had just exited. "Yeah, especially that," she said, nodding toward it.

Ramona didn't turn around. She just looked up toward the treetops. "The air is so fresh up here, I love it. I forget about the altitude now, but I could barely breathe for the first few weeks. I needed to take a rest just from brushing my teeth."

Cody laughed. She had definitely been feeling pretty zapped.

"Anyway, it's not meant to be intimidating here," Ramona continued. "The Ark is just a place where we can all feel safe. A place where Ones can be proud about what makes us special. A place where we can keep that progress going forward."

"I'm actually not a One. Technically, I mean." Cody hadn't planned on being so forthcoming with this stranger, but Ramona seemed trustworthy, and it was a relief to get it off her chest. She knew people would find out anyway.

Ramona looked at her quizzically. "What do you mean?"

"I thought I was. I was told that I was for my whole life. And then—"

"Edith," Ramona said quickly. She looked intently at Cody. "You weren't on the List."

"Exactly. It was a pretty big surprise."

"Well, you certainly look like a One. And if Kai brought you all the way up to this place and Edith is letting you stay, I'm sure there's a good reason for you to be here."

Cody thought about that for a second. Why exactly was she at the Ark? She had committed herself to fighting for the Ones, and apparently this was the best place to do it, and also her best chance at helping James. At least that's what Kai said.

Or was it just that Kai and Taryn wanted to keep an eye on her now that Cody knew their secrets? It was hard to know.

Cody had to remind herself that without Kai, without the New Weathermen, she would still be alone in Shasta, fighting pointlessly with Ms. Bixley and her idiot classmates and screaming into the wind. She had to trust that this was the place where she could really accomplish something that mattered.

"So . . . what do you think of Edith?" Ramona asked. "She must have really changed your life, I bet."

Cody could barely answer that question herself. And even with Ramona's warmth, Cody stopped herself from spilling her guts about Edith Vale. She remembered that she was the outsider here. The only non-One. The newest member of the community. The least informed and the least important. Ramona seemed trustworthy, but Cody wasn't ready to test that.

"What Edith did was brilliant," Cody said assertively. "I really like her."

=

Whatever Cody really thought about Edith Vale, she was open to changing it as she walked to dinner that night. Edith hadn't answered Cody's question about releasing the List, but she had promised a story instead. It would take a pretty powerful yarn to change Cody's mind. Dropping the List on the Internet like a secret new album had sowed havoc; what could possibly justify that?

Following Kai's lead along the wooded trail, the two made their way to what Edith had identified as the mess hall. At least a dozen other Ones from around the compound were also streaming toward it. Before they reached the entrance, Kai slowed and leaned into Cody.

"Remember, you're new here. Try to make a good impression," he said.

"What's that supposed to mean?" Cody asked.

"I know you think you're in charge of whatever room you're standing in. I respect that. I'm the same way," Kai said. "But neither of us is in charge here. Edith is."

They reached the mess hall, and Kai held the door for her. Cody was about to respond to him, but she was instantly overwhelmed; for the first time in days, she could actually smell food. She practically knocked Kai over trying to get inside.

Laid out on a giant wood table were several steaming pots of stew—dark, chunky, and fragrant. Cody rushed to take a seat, finding an empty bowl at the place setting in front of her. With all her willpower, she refrained from serving herself immediately. *Make a good impression*, she remembered. She needed these people to help her save James.

As everyone else came inside and sat down, Cody

looked around the table, which was lit by the dim glow of gas lamps. There were about twenty other Ones there, all a little older than Cody and appearing like they'd been stuck in the mountains for a while. In other words, it looked like an advertisement from a trendy camping catalog. Everyone was strong, healthy, and beautiful in their own way. And they had a seriousness that reminded Cody of her first meeting with the New Weathermen. These were Ones who had chosen to devote their lives to fighting the Equality Movement.

Suddenly, Cody felt someone standing over her. "That's where Edith sits," a voice growled.

She looked up into the face of a glaring twenty-year-old whose muscles were straining the seams of his flannel shirt. Cody felt all eyes turn to her.

"Oh, I didn't realize," she said, and started to stand.

But before she could get up, Edith breezed into the mess hall and placed a hand on Cody's elbow, imploring her to stay seated.

"Don't be silly, it's fine," Edith said. She cast her eyes toward the flannel-clad piece of granite who'd admonished Cody. "Cooper likes to keep everyone organized here. Thank you, Cooper, I'll just sit right here."

Cooper nodded obediently and circled around to the other side of the table. Edith took the seat next to Cody, and everyone immediately clasped hands.

"Ones first, to the last," they all declared in unison.

Finally, people started serving themselves. Cody tried to wait politely—she managed to let three people go ahead of her—before gleefully savoring her first bite and then cramming her mouth to capacity. It was a glorious feeling.

Of course, while she was chewing, Edith turned to her. "You had a question for me, right? About the List?"

Cody managed to nod.

"Before I answer that, you should know who I really am," Edith said. She paused, and Cody felt herself lean in, rapt. "As far as I know, I am the first One ever born."

Cody gulped, both from the mouthful of food and the bombshell. Edith couldn't be a One, she thought. The National Institutes of Health only started their program twenty years earlier. Edith was twice that old, at least. Whenever Edith was born, there was no such thing as Ones.

"My parents were both scientists. Geneticists, in fact. And they really wanted to have a baby, but they couldn't get pregnant. It was while I was being conceived in vitro that they just couldn't help themselves. They took the little embryo version of me and made a few changes. Maybe more than a few, actually." Edith laughed. "You would never believe that they're my real parents. . . . They look just as dorky as they sound."

Cody leaned back and regarded Edith with a discerning eye for the first time. Yes, she was in her forties, but now Cody could see the genetic engineering at work: the perfect facial symmetry, the thick hair, the dark green eyes, the athletic build. Cody would have noticed it sooner, but she had never seen a One so old before. That meant Edith wasn't subject to the guessing game that everyone played with members of Cody's generation.

"When I was a little kid, my parents kept everything a secret," Edith said. "But as I was growing up, the debate over genetic engineering exploded. We finally had the ability to do it easily. Some people wanted to explore it; others wanted it banned. The NIH pilot program was set in motion as a compromise of sorts. And there I was, the only genetically engineered teenager."

Cody took all this in with amazement. Edith Vale was the first genetically modified baby. It sounded crazy, but somehow it also seemed to fit with her growing picture of Edith. And Cody couldn't help but feel a pang of sympathy.

"So how did you find out?" Cody asked. She thought back to her own moments of discovery: her mother explaining to Cody that she was a One, and what that meant—and later, the shattering moment of identity theft when Cody discovered it was all a lie.

"My parents eventually told me when I was around your age, and I freaked out. Just by virtue of the fact that we had to keep it a secret, I knew that being modified was a threat to the rest of society. I understood why, of course, but I also sensed how ugly it might get. So, by myself, I set the wheels in motion for what I called the Locust Project."

Cody noticed some of the Ones around the table nodding with pride. Then Edith locked eyes with her, and she could feel Edith's intensity building.

"Locusts mature underground and out of sight for seventeen years until they finally emerge and nurture the next generation. So that's what I did. I went to college and took all the right classes and applied for all the right jobs. I didn't know exactly how I was going to do it, but I had to find a way. I saw the rise of the Equality Movement, and I knew I might be the only hope for stopping it. Eventually I saw an angle at the National Security Agency. I began to work there, and I kept my head down and my nose clean. I started getting promotions. I got higher clearance. And I knew, somewhere in that NSA database, there was a comprehensive list of every genetically engineered baby born through the NIH program."

Edith paused, clearly overwhelmed at the memory of her long struggle. Cody could sense all the other Ones were locked in on their conversation. There were no other conversations at the table, and even the clanking of utensils had gone silent. Somehow the soft yellow light from the lamps all seemed to shine on Edith. Cody snuck a glance at Kai, who was just as rapt as everyone else.

And then Edith gathered herself. "You asked me earlier why I did it?"

Cody nodded.

"Progress is never earned without a fight, Cody. Now it's finally time for the Ones to join this battle and get our freedom back. The List was my wake-up call to all the other locusts."

Cody felt chills creep down her back. It was thrilling to learn that she and the New Weathermen were not just a desperate ragtag militia thrown together by chance—they were actually part of a grand plan. While the world was playing checkers over the issue of genetic engineering, Edith Vale had snuck off with a chessboard and set up the pieces for her own game.

"So that brings us to you now," Edith said, focusing on Cody. "Are you willing to do whatever it takes to save the Ones from annihilation? Are you ready to swear to put Ones first?"

"Yes, I am," Cody said firmly. "But first I need to rescue James from the detention camp."

"We don't have personal agendas here, Cody. The camps are obviously a problem. But we can't solve that right now. That's not the plan."

"That's my plan," Cody said. She looked at Kai across the table. His glare implored her to stand down.

Edith narrowed her eyes at Cody. "There's only one plan

here. I've been working on it for decades, and everyone else at this table agrees with it. We are going to fight for our freedom and take our rightful spot in this world. So you can either join us or leave."

Before Cody could answer, Kai cleared his throat and jumped in. "I think what Cody means is that she wants to focus on freeing the camps *as soon as possible*. She didn't mean to suggest—"

"No, I meant right away," Cody said.

She appreciated Kai sticking his neck out for her, but he wasn't going to change her mind, and now she just hoped he'd be quiet. Cody had come to the Ark to get help in liberating James. That wasn't up for debate.

"Cody, I think that's admirable," Edith said. "But we can't help you. There are operations in place that are much more significant. We can't afford to jeopardize them."

Cody realized this wasn't a debate for Edith, either. She was never going to be won over by Cody's appeals to save a single, specific One. Cody needed more than an argument. She needed a trump card.

"I'm not asking for your help. I'm insisting on it," she said, a plan beginning to take shape in her head.

"Excuse me?"

There were gasps from the Ones around the table. Clearly no one talked to Edith Vale like this, let alone delivered an ultimatum.

"I'm here to make a deal," Cody said. "You have something I want—a determined strike force ready and able to raid the camps and free the Ones held inside. And I have something you want. Let's trade."

"What do you have that I want?" Edith asked skeptically.

Cody was committed now. She had to keep going. So she put everything she had into her performance.

"You know that I was captured by the Equality agents. You know that I was detained. You know that I spent time with Agent Norton. Lots of time."

Edith nodded, still wary. "Yes. I know all of that."

"And because of that experience, I know something about Agent Norton that can change this entire war. Something that can help us win. Something that you need to hear."

Edith glared at Cody. "What could you possibly know?"

"It's about Agent Norton and it's about you. She's obsessed with you. And I know exactly how she's going to catch you, the trap that she's laying for you." Cody stared at Edith and tried to speak as firmly as possible. "And I'm only going to tell you after you help me free James."

As everyone else looked on in shock, Cody saw Edith do the calculation in her head, saw the desperate self-interest overwhelm her beautiful, genetically perfect face. Cody knew she had her on the hook.

The bluff had worked.

CHAPTER 4

KAI COULDN'T BELIEVE what he had witnessed in the mess hall. No one talked to Edith like that. No one negotiated with her. No one defied her orders. Kai had watched people slink away from her after a single look. And yet Cody had been at the Ark for all of five hours and had gone toe-to-toe with her.

When they got back to the bunkhouse, Kai wheeled on Cody.

"That was insane."

"I'm not crazy, I'm determined," Cody said.

"Determined to get booted out of here?"

Cody didn't respond.

"You have to apologize to Edith. Maybe she'll let you stay."

A few other Ones had trickled into the bunkhouse—

Taryn, Ramona, and a quiet guy Kai had met before named Gabriel. They were all watching him and Cody.

"Nice table manners," Taryn said to Cody as she passed by.

"Do you really know what trap Agent Norton is setting for Edith?" Gabriel asked. He looked disgusted that Cody would keep such information to herself. The residents of the Ark had a very clear idea of how they should all behave, and there was no room for undermining Edith in the name of individual ambition.

"Yeah, I do," she said. "It's something Edith would really love to know."

Kai shook his head, aggravated that Cody kept riling everyone up.

Ramona put an arm around her shoulder. "I don't agree with what you're doing, but I still think it's very romantic. You want to get your man back. Who can blame you?"

"Thank you, Ramona," Cody said, then smiled at Kai. "See? Why would I apologize to Edith? We struck a deal and everything is fine."

Kai took hold of Cody's wrist and led her out of the bunkhouse. "Come on, let's talk outside."

Cody reluctantly trudged along behind him as they headed off the trail and into the woods.

When Kai thought no one could hear them, he spun around to face Cody. "Look, I get why you did it. And fine,

49

forget about the apology. But at least tell Edith the info now. Maybe she'll still go along with the raid."

"Kai, I can't tell her now. That's not how leverage works."

"Cody, you don't want to threaten her like this. You are going to turn her into an enemy."

"She and I both want the same thing. We can't be enemies."

Kai was silent for a moment. It was true that Cody and Edith both wanted to fight for the Ones. But he knew their respective visions of how to win that battle were drastically different.

Cody hadn't learned that yet. And Kai was afraid to tell her.

He was also angry that Cody had dragged him into the middle of this. Kai had brought her to the Ark and introduced her to Edith. If Cody was hell-bent on getting on the wrong side of Edith, that wasn't going to fly with him.

So Kai considered a different way to resolve the situation. "Tell me, at least. Tell me what Agent Norton told you."

"So you can run and tell Edith?"

"No. So I know you're serious."

"You don't believe me?"

"I wouldn't put it past you."

Cody glared at him.

"Relax, that's a compliment," he said. "You want something badly, and you'll do anything to get it. I understand."

Cody looked at him curiously. "You do?"

"Sure."

"What have you ever wanted that badly?" she asked softly.

Kai turned away ever so slightly, but he could feel Cody noticing. Her question caught him off guard. He knew what the obvious answer was: victory for the Ones. His desire for that consumed every minute of his life. But part of him wondered if there was anything else he felt passionately about. He had a vague sense a new obsession was building inside him, something even more uncontrollable than his passion for the Ones, something he was still too scared to talk about.

But he realized that he was being foolish—one desire had to take priority. And for Kai, that would always be fighting for the Ones.

Cody prodded him. "Besides this cause, I mean—what else do you want?"

Kai sensed that Cody could imagine his answer better than he could. She was challenging him to find it, and the look in her eyes was the same look they'd shared at the top of the quarry, almost overrun by the Equality Team. This time, though, they weren't going to be interrupted. This time, Kai simply turned away.

"Nothing, I guess," he said.

Cody pulled back from him, and Kai thought he saw the faintest sign of disappointment on her face.

"So then you can't relate," she said. "Which means you can save your advice."

Cody turned and walked away through the trees, leaving Kai alone, staring after her.

═

Early the next morning, Kai had to face the moment he knew was inevitable. Edith stood right in front of him, looked him in the eyes, and asked him point-blank.

"Is Cody telling the truth?"

They were inside the armory, surrounded by tall shelves of guns and other weaponry. Flanking Edith were Taryn, Cooper, and Ramona—the Ark's informal leadership council.

Over the past couple of years, Kai had taken on the role of leading external missions. It was a distinguished position, obviously, but it meant that he wasn't at their home base as much as the others.

Cooper was in charge of security for the Ark. A proud Texan, he was an avid military historian who lived for the Second Amendment. He had taken Taryn under his wing the last time they were here together, and now she helped him maintain their stockpile.

Ramona was Edith's most trusted confidante. A child prodigy from Maine who had already completed medical school, she was a talented doctor and scientist, and the only other person who knew all the details about Edith's special project.

And now all of them were waiting for Kai to answer.

"I believe her," he finally spit out.

"I don't care if you believe her," Edith responded. "Do you know for a fact that she has intelligence that can help us?"

Kai waited a moment, then shook his head. He wasn't even sure he wanted to lie for Cody and confirm that she had something to offer, but he knew what would happen next—they would insist he reveal it, which was a perfectly reasonable demand. And then he'd be stuck.

"I told you," Cooper said to Edith. "She's just bluffing because she wants our help. She's going to get us all killed."

"Are you saying we can't successfully raid one of the camps?" Kai asked. "What's the point of all these weapons, then?"

Cooper jumped to get in Kai's face, but Edith stepped between them.

"These weapons are in case we have to defend ourselves," Edith said. "They're not meant for suicide missions."

Ramona looked at Taryn. "You've been around her, Taryn. Do you trust this girl? I can already tell it's no use asking Kai."

Kai tried to catch Taryn's eye before she answered. He knew she hated Cody and had some legitimate reasons to doubt her. But James had saved Taryn's butt, too.

"She's lied to us before and can't be trusted," Taryn said. "It's been like that since the moment I met her."

Some character witness, Kai thought as he hung his head. He realized he'd never be able to prove that Cody was telling the truth. He didn't know the answer himself. But he was also pissed that this was what they were focusing on. Ones were getting rounded up into camps, and they were just going to sit around and do nothing? Cody's honesty was beside the point now—Kai wanted to go notch a victory for the Ones.

"Who cares about what Cody says? Let's take down the camp anyway," he said.

"To what end?" Edith asked.

"To show that the Ones are still fighting," Kai said. "To make a statement to the rest of the country. To stop our fellow Ones from getting the Vaccine before it's too late. Isn't that what we're supposed to be doing? Or did you all forget that while you've been cooped up in the mountains?"

Kai could see that even Taryn and Cooper agreed with him a little. Ramona didn't seem moved. Edith shared a look with her before speaking.

"We're too close on another project to suffer a setback," she said.

Kai thought he knew what Edith was referring to. But even as part of her inner circle, he didn't know everything. And he was smart enough not to press her; Edith wouldn't tolerate that.

So Kai took a different tack. "Edith, think about how

powerful this will look. Think about everyone in the country discovering that Ones won't stand for these camps."

Kai saw Edith perk up a bit, and he kept going. "I promise there won't be a setback. Give me a couple people to help, and I'll do it with Cody. It'll be a huge propaganda victory for us. And then, immediately after, we'll get to hear her intel about Norton."

As Edith considered his plea, Kai felt his excitement growing. This could truly be a perfect mission for him to lead. He would redeem himself for his defeat at the quarry. He would strike an important blow against the Equality Movement. He would prove to Edith how valuable he was.

Finally, Edith nodded, almost imperceptibly. "I agree it would be a nice coup for us. But if you fail, you won't make it back here. You might miss out on something . . . something I can't fully explain right now." She paused for a moment. "Are you willing to take that risk?"

If Edith was telling the truth, if she really was getting close on the project that Kai had only heard rumors about, then he truly would regret missing it. But the Ones would never win the fight by playing it safe. Kai knew that, and more important, he knew he had a responsibility to keep demonstrating that. This was the role he played in their movement, and he had always embraced it. This was why he was part of the leadership council. Raiding the camp was worth the risk.

He met Edith's gaze and nodded. "I'm doing it. And I'm coming back."

=

With their predawn meeting adjourned, Kai made his way back to the bunkhouse. As he walked briskly through the cold alpine air, he heard a shout from behind him.

"Hey!"

It was Taryn. Kai slowed so she could catch up with him.

"Why are you doing this?" she asked.

"Doing what?"

"Risking everything for her. Not listening to anyone else. Defying Edith."

"Taryn, it's a good plan; we're going to—"

"Forget the plan. I'm talking about *her*! She's got you all messed up."

"Cody? She's got nothing to do with it."

"You've got your head stuck so far up your ass, it's liver-adjacent."

Kai was angry now. "Where's your head, then? The federal government has rounded up all the Ones and locked them away in detention camps. I want to break into one and destroy it. What exactly is wrong with that?"

"You're doing it for her. So she'll think you're a hero."

Kai scoffed. "Get out of my face with that garbage. Cody can think whatever she wants; I couldn't care less. I'm doing it for the Ones who are stuck there, getting the Vaccine."

Taryn just shook her head. "Have fun believing that. But take it from someone who's known you for a long time: If you're not careful, that girl is going to be the end of you."

Too aggravated to respond, Kai spun and walked away. He didn't have the energy to argue with Taryn. At least he knew this wasn't about any romantic feelings she had for him, or any guy for that matter. Her protests weren't the longings of a jealous rival; they were misguided attempts to preserve a partnership that was truly special.

Since they had met years ago in a reform school, Kai and Taryn had agreed on one thing: Their fight for the Ones took precedence over everything else. And more significantly, they shared a theory about relationships that had been beaten into them: Love is never real. Kai had learned it in his dozens of foster families and group homes. For Taryn, growing up in a nice Christian home hadn't stopped her from learning the same ugly lesson. One day her parents discovered their made-to-order daughter actually had her own identity, one that clashed with their values, and they kicked her out of the house. The lower expectations that Kai and Taryn developed made them better revolutionaries, and they reveled in that advantage.

But Kai could tell Taryn thought he was losing his edge.

He usually trusted her instincts, so it was scary to hear her warning. He'd just have to prove her wrong, and show Edith, too, by leading this camp siege. He laughed to himself about Taryn's warning that Cody would somehow destroy him. Kai knew there was an unavoidable live-fast-die-young element to his life, but his odds weren't made any worse by the existence of Cody.

Back at the bunkhouse now, Kai entered and saw Cody asleep on her bed. She'd want to know the news, of course, but he wasn't so eager to update her. Kai didn't want to give the impression that Cody could simply snap her fingers and everyone at the Ark would fall in line.

A moment later, however, Taryn walked in and let the door slam loudly behind her. Cody stirred awake and looked up at them.

"Aren't you going to tell her?" Taryn asked Kai coolly.

"Tell me what?" Cody asked.

"Edith approved the mission," Kai said. "We're taking down the camp."

Cody gasped, then she jumped out of bed and wrapped her arms around Kai.

"Thank you, Kai. I owe you."

Kai slid out of the embrace as Taryn glared at him.

"How did you convince Edith?" Cody asked.

"I just told her that she could trust you. That you'll give her the intel about Norton. And regardless, we should destroy every one of these camps anyway."

For an instant, the look on Cody's face made him think that he'd gotten something wrong. She looked reluctant, even afraid. Kai didn't understand it, but then the look was gone.

"Do you think we'll be able to pull it off?" she asked.

"Destroying the camp? Yeah, if we're smart. Cooper has plenty of tricks up his sleeve."

"I meant saving James."

Kai was reminded again that Cody's top priority wasn't the same as his. For him, every other One in that camp was just as important as James.

"It's only been a few days," Kai said. "With a little bit of luck, he'll walk right out of there with us."

Cody smiled at him and then almost burst with excitement. "When do we leave?"

=

Cody's enthusiasm aside, they couldn't actually leave until they had a planning session later that afternoon. Kai had spent the day considering the best way to carry out the raid. When the time came, he led Cody to the armory, where they met up with Taryn, Cooper, and Gabriel, who were going to join them on the mission. They gathered around a table, and Kai stepped to the head.

"The five of us are going to pull this off. But we need to be smart, fast, and ruthless."

He unrolled a map of Northern California and pointed at an area within the boundaries of a state park. "The camp is in the woods here. These places are not fortresses. They are designed to keep everyone inside, not to withstand a siege. Cooper, this is all you. How do you want to get inside?"

Cooper looked at the map and thought for a moment. "We can hike up to its perimeter and wait for darkness. I can lay down as many explosives as we can carry. We'll blow out the bases of any guard towers and punch a hole in the fence."

Kai listened, wheels turning.

Cooper went on. "Once we breach the camp, we disperse and blow every locked door we find. They'll be shooting at us by now, so we return fire and move quickly from cover to cover. Trust me, we got the guns here to answer back just fine. The sooner we get all them kids stampeding, the better. Set off a few flash grenades and smoke bombs on the way out, disable their vehicles, and then scamper like hell through the woods."

"And then what? Where are all of them going to go?" Cody asked. "The Ones in the camp, I mean."

"They'll figure it out," Cooper said. "We'll try to lead as many of them as possible back here. The rally point is at the train tracks. Catch the midnight express right back to the Cascades."

"We doing this with night vision?" Gabriel asked.

Cooper shook his head. "No need. That place will be lit up like a shopping mall."

A silence fell over the table. Kai hadn't chimed in yet; he was still deep in thought. He finally looked up from the map.

"It's not going to work," he said, shaking his head.

Cooper straightened up, offended. "What's the problem?"

"The only way we pull this off is if we get into the camp undetected. We have too much work to do on the inside, getting everyone out of the barracks. If the guards hear us coming in, they'll have plenty of time to mount a defense. It could be a slaughter."

"So how do we get inside?" Gabriel asked.

Kai didn't have an answer yet. He stepped away from the table and began pacing around the small armory.

"What if we let ourselves be captured?" Cody suggested. "Then we could organize the breakout from the inside."

Kai laughed. "Trust me, if they ever get their hands on this crew, we're not going to some run-of-the-mill internment camp."

He stopped his pacing and stared out the window, taking in the unending vista of trees. "We have to get in silently. Quickly. Without causing any—" Kai cut himself off. He started bounding around the armory, opening all the weapon lockers, looking for something.

"Dude, what are you doing?" Taryn asked.

Kai kept searching furiously. The rest of the crew

watched him, confused. Finally, he found it. He pulled out a crossbow and turned to face them.

"Follow me."

He stepped outside, the others following, and pointed up to the treetops towering above them.

"The camp is in a state park filled with giant sequoia trees. We get to the top of the trees and we zip-line in."

As everyone stared up into the canopy of pines, Kai thrust the crossbow toward Cooper. "Can you attach a rope to this arrow? Maybe a hundred yards long?"

"Sure, no problem," Cooper said.

"Can you fire it accurately to hit the side of a building or a wall?"

Cooper looked to Taryn. She nodded.

Kai smiled. "Then we are going to float right into that camp, quiet as a moth."

"What about harnesses?" Gabriel asked. "We don't have proper climbing gear here. How are we actually going to ride the zip line?"

Gabriel was kind of annoying with all his questions, but Kai was grateful that Edith had assigned him to the mission. He was quiet and calm, the type of worrier every group needed. And as for how to ride the zip line, Kai reached down and unbuckled his belt. He yanked it off with gusto, holding the buckle in front of everyone.

"We thread the rope through here," he said. "And then hold on tight."

Kai was met with a few ambivalent stares. But no one offered a better idea.

"All right, last question," Cody said. She took the crossbow from Cooper. "Will this thing actually hold our body weight?"

Kai looked at her with a gleam in his eye. "Let's find out."

Twenty minutes later, Kai was holding on for dear life to the top of a pine tree. The climb had been relatively simple, but now that he was fifty feet in the air, he was swaying in the wind, and the ground seemed very far away.

Kai took a deep breath and shifted the crossbow off his shoulder. They had secured some climbing rope to it, which was now coiled up in a backpack. Kai found the other end of the rope, slipped it through his metal belt buckle and began tying it securely around the trunk of the tree. He made a few extra knots, just in case.

At last, Kai was ready to fire the crossbow. He looked down over the expanse of the Ark and saw the armory building, with the rest of the mission crew standing off to the side. Kai steadied himself, aimed the crossbow, and fired its arrow. It struck squarely into the side of the building with minimal sound. He was getting more and more confident that his plan might actually work.

Kai took another minute to pull the rope taut. Then he grabbed hold of his dangling belt, pulling down to test his weight on it. Strong enough, he reasoned. He jumped from the tree and hoped for the best. Immediately, he was gliding down toward the Ark, moving quickly but with enough friction so that he wasn't out of control. And the zip line and arrow were holding.

Along the way, Kai took in a bird's-eye view of their compound and had a moment of profound appreciation for everything they'd accomplished at the Ark. Flying over some unsuspecting people, Kai couldn't contain his excitement.

"Ones first, motherfuckers!" he shouted at the top of his lungs. The Ones below looked up in surprise.

A moment later, Kai realized he was about to crash into the wall of the armory. He tried to drag his feet along the ground, but that barely slowed his speed. He was going fast enough to break a leg or an arm—or a neck. At the last second before he slammed into the wall, Kai let go of the zip line and bounced along the ground, raising a cloud of dust. When he looked up, Cody, Taryn, Cooper, and Gabriel were standing around him.

"Works like a charm," he said, grinning. "Might want to tweak the landing protocol."

"I think that was user error," Cody said.

Kai got up and brushed himself off. He hadn't noticed that Edith had joined the group watching the test run. She stepped forward, taking note of the zip line strung over her head.

"Smart," she said. "So you're ready to go?"

Kai looked over at everyone and nodded. "Yeah. We're going to hike out of here at dawn."

"I'd like to say something before you leave."

Everyone turned to face Edith.

"If we are going to take this risk, it's important to remember exactly what's going on out there. Our brothers and sisters are imprisoned against their will. Locked behind fences like animals. And every day that goes by, more and more of them are being treated with the Vaccine. Changed forever. Diminished. Controlled." Edith paused here. "Unless we stop them. And we're their only hope."

Kai looked around. He could tell everyone was ready for this mission.

Then Edith added one more thing. "But beyond our cherished idea of Ones first, there's something more important to remember." Edith fixed her icy gaze on Cody and pointed straight at her. "Bring this one back alive."

Edith turned to face only Kai now. "Is that clear?" she asked.

Kai stared back at Edith, not answering for a moment. He could feel Cody's eyes on him. He had no idea what she would tell Edith when they returned, but that was her problem. All he could do was look at Edith and nod.

"Crystal clear."

CHAPTER 5

CODY KEPT REMINDING herself not to look down. She had climbed trees before, but none like this. It was an absolute monster, an ancient California sequoia that felt as tall as a skyscraper.

She tried to follow the route of Kai and Taryn above, and to go fast enough that Cooper and Gabriel wouldn't run into her from behind. It was hard to see, though—everyone was covered in black clothing that blended seamlessly into the dark forest, while the cloudy night sky overhead hid any traces of moonlight. And they didn't dare use flashlights so close to the camp. So Cody pressed onward as best she could from one precarious foothold to the next.

She could see the camp easily now in a clearing just in front of them. The ugly rectangle was illuminated by floodlights and surrounded by a tall chain-link fence topped with razor wire. There were a half-dozen simple wooden buildings in the middle of an open expanse and a few single-story brick structures along the edges. A three-story guard post loomed high at one of the camp's corners, its spotlight fortunately turned off at the moment.

Forty feet in the air now, Cody hugged the trunk as a gust of wind shook the tree like it was a feather. She was grateful for the sticky sap that was proving to be a useful safety feature. Pressed tight to the bark, Cody could feel the butt of her assault rifle jabbing into her stomach uncomfortably. It felt weird to be carrying such a power-ful weapon, one that she had never handled until a quick lesson on their train ride down to the camp. Cody knew it was a tool of powerful destruction, and it scared her a little bit. She wondered if she'd really be able to point it at the guards in the camp and let the bullets fly.

The stark reality of the scene below made Cody think that she could. She stared down at a government-operated internment camp, one of many around the country, where one percent of her generation was being held against their will. This wasn't a secret or some kind of outlier—this had somehow become an accepted reality in America. Citizens knew about it. Politicians approved it. Companies built it. Of course, the government portrayed the camps as comfortable havens where the Ones would be held only temporarily. But that was a contradiction in and of itself. Nowhere that people were held against their will was comfortable.

Especially a place that was administering the Vaccine.

The wind subsided, and Cody continued her climbing. Her anger was rising now, and she felt validated in her lie to Edith. So what if she didn't have any real intel about Agent Norton's plans? They were going to liberate this camp. They were going to save James. Whatever blowback Cody got for this manipulative ploy would be well worth it. She realized now, with growing confidence, that she would, in fact, be able to fire her gun.

Finally, just above her, Kai and Taryn stopped climbing. Cody joined them a moment later, and they perched in the highest branches, all staring down at the camp below them, silent, still, and peaceful—for now. Cody met Kai's eyes, and he shook his head in disgust at the scene below, echoing her thoughts.

"Thank you for getting us here," Cody whispered. She knew they wouldn't have this chance if Kai hadn't gone to bat for her.

He nodded. "I'm glad we're doing it."

Cooper and Gabriel caught up to them, and everyone began preparing their equipment. Taryn unshouldered the crossbow and took the gigantic coil of rope from Kai. She secured it to the arrow with a tight knot.

Binoculars raised to his eyes, Cooper instructed Taryn

on where to aim. "Do you see the broad backside of the building on the southern edge?"

Taryn nodded and pointed the crossbow at it.

"Are you sure you can hit that?" Kai asked.

She turned and glared at him, pissed that he'd ruined her concentration.

"Sorry," Kai said. "I'm just saying that if this arrow flops into the ground or lands somewhere outside the fence, we're screwed. Make it count."

"Good idea," Taryn said as she resumed lining up her shot.

Cody held her breath as Taryn finally pulled the trigger. The arrow soared silently toward the camp, a tail of rope trailing behind it. After what seemed like a full minute, the arrow struck the wall of the building. Everyone in the tree strained their eyes to see if any guards had noticed the disturbance. No—the camp remained lifeless.

Kai got to work quickly. He reached out to Cooper, who handed him five mismatched belts they had scavenged from people at the Ark. Kai slipped the rope through all the buckles, then pulled it as taut as possible and tied it around the tree trunk. The zip line was officially rigged.

Cooper, ready to go first, made his way to the line, gingerly stepping around people in the tree. He took hold of a belt and nodded back to them.

"See you in a bit," he said as he jumped out of the tree.

Cody watched him shoot down the line, seemingly

floating through the night toward the camp. He didn't seem to be going that fast, but when he passed just above the barbed wire and crashed onto the ground, Cody saw how much speed he'd picked up.

Taryn jumped on the line next, grabbing a belt and setting off from the tree. Cooper had secured the line inside the camp and was there to soften her landing. Gabriel went next without a hitch.

It was just Cody and Kai now in the tree. He held the line for her.

"You better hurry up," he said. "James is down there."

Cody smiled at him, oddly excited to jump out of a tree.

"Remember," Kai said, "hold the belt like this so all your weight isn't on your fingers."

Kai wrapped his arms in front of her and demonstrated on the belt, gripping it with both elbows at a right angle. All of a sudden, their bodies were pressed tightly against each other, and for the briefest moment, Cody couldn't deny the thrill of being on this mission with Kai. But just as quickly, she thought of James and felt guilty.

"Yeah, no kidding," Cody said, knocking Kai's arms away. "I know how gravity works."

Flustered, she launched herself from the tree in a rush, barreling downward out of control. As she gripped the belt tightly and kept her eyes locked on her landing spot, the wind whistled in her ears and her hair flew up behind her. She held out an absurd hope that maybe James was at a window somewhere in the camp, watching her dramatic arrival. Even if he smiled at this wonderful sight, he probably wouldn't approve, she thought.

Lost in this rescue fantasy, Cody forgot to keep her legs up, and just before hitting the ground her ankle clipped the razor wire on top of the fence. She immediately felt it tear through her clothing and slice her skin. As the searing pain reached her brain, Cody was caught by Cooper and Taryn. She fell to the ground, biting the sleeve of her coat to keep from screaming out in pain.

Taryn stood over Cody, looked down at her leg, already covered in blood, and held her finger to her mouth. The message was clear. Cody wasn't dying, and they had to stay quiet.

A moment later, Kai arrived on the zip line, and they were all inside the camp. Cody knelt down and tried to administer to the wound on her shin. She ripped off some of the torn pants fabric and wrapped it tightly as a bandage. Then she looked up at Kai and nodded. She'd be fine.

Cooper gestured across the camp at a line of security vehicles. He was going to set up remote mines to disable the cars and, in the back part of the camp, blow a hole through the fence. When all the Ones were out of the barracks, they'd escape through there. Cooper gave the rest of the team a thumbs-up and took off across the camp.

The rest of the Weathermen cautiously fanned out among the buildings in the center of the camp—the barracks that held the Ones. They knew they'd eventually draw the attention of the guards, but wanted to delay that as long as possible. Each of them eventually made it to the door of a barrack—all locked, as they suspected.

Cody watched as Kai pointed his gun at the nearest door. The rest of them followed suit, each aiming at a different barracks door. Kai raised his arm to get everyone's attention, using his fingers to count down from three. When he finished, Cody, Taryn, and Gabriel joined him in simultaneously firing, exploding the silence of the camp with gunfire.

Within seconds, alarms were ringing, emergency lights were flashing, and spotlights were dancing around the camp like panicked fireflies. Cody smashed through the doorway in front of her. As she stepped into the dark barrack, dozens of Ones stared back at her from two long rows of sparse cots. They looked frozen, incredulous.

"Come on, we gotta move!" Cody shouted. "Out the back fence and into the trees!"

Cody heard a major explosion from the back of the camp—Cooper had blown the hole in the fence. She stepped outside, ready to race to the next barrack. But she couldn't help herself from turning back and watching all the Ones run for the fence, clocking each of their faces. She was looking for James.

The guards had mobilized by now, and Cody saw a group rushing toward her, guns drawn. She heard a burst of gunfire from her left, and several of the guards fell down. Taryn was locked in on them.

"Keep going to the next building!" Taryn yelled in between bouts of covering fire.

Cody ran ahead and busted down the next door. The Ones here had a better sense of the escape plan and quickly began to rush outside. Cody watched their faces again as they raced past. Lots of tall, healthy, good-looking teenage boys in identical uniforms. Each one could have been James, but she didn't spot him.

Before they all ran outside, Cody grabbed the last one.

"Wait!" she screamed over the din of the shooting and the alarms.

The kid, maybe a fourteen-year-old boy, stopped and looked at her. Cody could sense his desperation to keep moving, and she felt guilty for putting him at risk. But she had to find James.

"Do you know James Livingston? Do you know where he is?"

The kid shook his arm free. "He's gone; they took him away," he said, then sprinted for the door and joined the stampede of Ones moving for the back fence.

Gone? What did that mean?

Cody ran after him, but there was no hope of catching him. The camp was a battlefield now, with bullets whizzing everywhere. *They took him away.* Was James somewhere else in the camp? The brick buildings at the entrance looked more secure than the barracks. Maybe he'd been locked up in there. She had to find out.

She moved forward, ducking in between the barracks, heading for the entrance of the camp.

"Cody, this way!" Kai shouted to her from behind. "We got everyone out—let's go!"

Cody ignored him and kept moving. She sprinted across an open expanse and felt shots from the guards whistle past her. There was a doorway just ahead of her, and she began firing at it as she ran, then plowed into it with her shoulder. The door flew open, and Cody bounced violently onto the floor of a long hallway, new waves of pain emanating from her leg.

She scrambled to her feet and inched ahead. The lights in the building were flashing and the sprinkler system was spraying water. As she moved along the corridor, Cody got her bearings and realized she was in the camp's medical building. There were shelves of first-aid equipment, and as she kicked open doors, she saw rooms that looked equipped for medical procedures.

And then Cody realized with horror—this wasn't some version of the nurse's office. This was where they administered the Vaccine.

Rage and nausea overwhelmed her as she imagined Ones being dragged in here against their will to have their lives changed. She was suddenly terrified that even if she did find James here, it might be too late.

THWACK!

A bullet popped into the wall just above her head. Cody spun around to see three guards racing toward her. She jumped into one of the medical rooms and was relieved to find another doorway, leading deeper into the building.

She rushed through room after room, hearing heavy footsteps behind her. The pounding of her pursuers combined with the shrieking alarms to create an echo chamber of mayhem. There was no sign of James, and no sign of an exit.

Cody's dash through the building eventually came to a dead end. She was stuck in a large office, with no escape from the guards closing in. Resolved to make a last stand, Cody took up a position behind a desk, leveled her gun on top of it, and knelt down low for cover. If the guards burst in through the door like idiots, she might be able to mow them all down. She would have to.

They didn't run in like idiots, though. Cody heard them reach the threshold and stay clear of the open doorway. One of them ducked his head in to peek inside the office. Cody fired but not quickly enough.

"Drop your weapon now!" came a shout.

Cody almost smiled. No one who walked through this house of horrors would ever give herself up voluntarily. These people couldn't give her the Vaccine, of course, but Cody remembered the other torments they could put her through. She kept her gun trained at the doorway.

A guard jumped across the threshold and fired several shots. Cody ducked and fired back. This wasn't much of a strategy, she realized, but she didn't have many choices. Cody knew she might hold her position for a little while, but there was no way out. She consoled herself by thinking of the crew from the Ark, safe in the woods by now with the Ones from the camp. Maybe James was with them; the kid she'd asked could have just been confused. Maybe this whole mission was a success—except for her getting pinned down in this building like the amateur she was.

Another volley of shots landed in the desk concealing her. Cody waited a second, then peeked over the edge, ready to return fire. The doorway was empty, but she kept her gun pointed at it.

Suddenly, three quick shots rang out. But Cody didn't duck. The guards weren't in the doorway. The shots weren't aimed at her. They came from the other room.

"Cody! Are you all right?" Kai's voice called out from behind a wall.

"Kai?"

"Don't shoot me, okay?"

Cody stayed hunkered down behind the desk. She couldn't believe this was happening. But there he was, stepping into the office, gun slung over his shoulder.

"Are you hurt?"

She shook her head.

"Then let's go already!" He nodded for Cody to get up and start moving.

"The guards?"

"Dead. Now come on."

Cody stood and peeked into the other room. Three bodies lay slumped on the floor. As Cody gazed down at their lifeless bodies, she was reminded again about the grave reality of this fight. The New Weathermen talked a lot about "life or death," but it was still a shock to her when that cliché actually came true.

Snapping out of her daze, Cody looked up at Kai. She was no longer trapped, but she still didn't want to just run off for the woods.

"James might be in here," she said. "I've got to keep looking."

Kai glared at her. "If you don't leave now, you're going to get captured. And I'm not coming back here again." He didn't even wait for a response, just took off sprinting back through the building.

Cody hesitated, but she knew he was right. There was no more time to aimlessly search for James. She just had to make it out of the camp and hope for the best. Even if James still needed her help, she had to help herself first.

She sprinted after Kai down a long hallway toward the building's back exit. She took a few glances out the windows and saw the camp still in chaos: lights flashing, fires burning, guards racing.

Cody caught up with Kai. They slammed together through the outer doorway and kept running. Kai tried to lead them into the darker shadows, as Cody heard guards yelling behind them. Gunshots crackled over her head. She spun her gun around and fired back blindly.

Finally they reached the back gate and darted through the smoldering hole Cooper had blown open. The tree line was only forty yards away, but it was uphill. Cody kicked her stride into her last gear and went past Kai, ignoring the pain in her shin. She ran ahead into the woods, veering every which way to avoid the trees. But she kept her pace and heard Kai following close behind.

When they had put some distance between themselves and the camp, Cody slowed down and tried to catch her breath. With their vehicles disabled, the guards would have to chase them on foot. Kai stared into the woods, listening intently. It sounded like they were free and clear.

"Thank you," Cody said when she could finally talk.

Kai nodded, still on full alert. "Come on, we need to get to the train tracks."

He started off again without another word. Cody was left wondering how he knew where she had gone in the camp. He must have been keeping an eye on her. It was true that she wasn't exactly a trained revolutionary like the rest of the Ones at the Ark, but she still resented being treated like the weak link. It was hard to argue about that right now, though. When she'd messed up and needed his help, he was there.

They hiked for several miles deeper into the woods. Neither knew for sure if they would reconnect with everyone from the camp. But Kai was confident that almost everyone had gotten away. The breakout had been a success.

The train they planned to catch curved on a path north through the foothills of the Sierra Nevadas. There were several places where it had to slow down for a particularly sharp bend. Cody and Kai finally made it to the rally point, and they discovered dozens of Ones huddled in the trees right next to the curving tracks.

"Did you guys stay for a tour or something?" Taryn asked, reclining against a tree.

Cody walked past her, scanning every face of the Ones sprawled out on the ground in their simple, camp-issued blue uniforms. After a full loop, she didn't see James. She made it back to Taryn.

"Is James here?"

"I didn't see him," Taryn said.

Cody walked back through the kids. "Do any of you know James Livingston? Was he in the camp?"

She went down the line of Ones, trying to make sure each one heard her.

"James Livingston? Do you know him?" she asked over and over.

Cody was finding only blank, exhausted looks, until suddenly a tall, broad-shouldered boy with scruffy black hair emerged from the back.

"Are you Cody?" he asked tentatively.

She rushed up to him. "Yes. Do you know James?"

He nodded but couldn't help casting his eyes down.

"Yeah. I'm Nicholas. . . . I rode the bus into camp next to him," the boy said.

"Where is he? Was he in the camp with the rest of you?"

"Yeah, he was with us. From the moment we arrived, he was trying to organize us to fight back. He kept telling us they were going to give us some vaccine or something. We didn't really know what to believe."

Cody grabbed Nicholas by the shoulders. "What happened to him?" she said sternly.

"He was right," Nicholas said. "They did want to do some procedure on us. But they couldn't just do it all at once. Before we could stage a breakout, they were onto him. Singled him out and took him away to go first."

Cody felt tears pool up in her eyes. Of course after discovering James had set the forest fire, Norton and the Equality agents would want to make an example out of him.

"He fought like hell to avoid it," Nicholas said. "They were dragging him, beating on him. They told the rest of

80

us to take note. They said it wasn't that bad, and that there was an easy way to go through it or a hard way. James took the hard way, obviously."

As Cody felt her body go numb, she realized there was a possible end to this story that was worse than James getting the Vaccine.

"He fought too hard during the procedure, I guess. We saw him get dragged into the med building, and then a few hours later they took him out in a body bag." Nicholas paused. "He's . . . he's dead. I'm sorry."

Cody crumpled into herself as the universe pressed down on her chest. She let out a wordless moan that descended into a wail and then petered out to a pathetic gasp.

James was dead.

She was too late to save him. He had been there to rescue her, and now she had failed him.

Nicholas looked down at her, his eyes tearing up, too. "He told me to look out for someone named Cody. He said you might come. And he wanted you to have something."

Nicholas pulled a twisted piece of fabric from his waistband. He extended his arm to give it to Cody. She grabbed it and unfurled the ball of cloth.

It was a piece of a uniform shirt from the camp. Everyone else surrounding Cody was wearing one, each with an ID number printed over the left breast. But what was left of James's shirt was different. He had crossed out the camp number with a black marker. And above that, scrawled in thick, defiant lettering, he had written something new.

PQ3318.

It was the catalog code that marked the spot in the school library where Cody and James had first kissed. And now it was his final message to her.

CHAPTER 6

KAI WATCHED CODY crumple to the ground, clutching what was left of James's shirt to her face. The Ones around her stood in silence. The only sound came from the quiet life of the forest and Cody's sobs.

As Kai stood off to the side, he was almost paralyzed by the pit growing in his stomach. The weird sensation had been with him since the middle of the raid, when Cody disappeared alone into the medical building. Against all his instincts and the strict plan he'd laid out, Kai couldn't stop himself from going after her. He knew she was putting herself in danger. But he also knew if he didn't follow, he might never see her again. And he knew he didn't want that.

Even so, Kai was freaked out that he had so easily diverted from his plan once Cody needed help. It was dangerous for him to lose his discipline like that, and he knew the others would take notice.

Now, seeing Cody in pain like this, Kai felt the urge to rush toward her again. But he stood frozen, scared to admit what this feeling really meant. Something more powerful than sympathy was bursting within him, and Kai knew he couldn't control it. Without consciously deciding to, he was suddenly kneeling next to Cody, embracing her, feeling her body heave into his. She dug her hands into his back, buried her head in his neck, and held on to him for dear life.

Even as he wished so badly to relieve her anguish, Kai couldn't help but consider the new world he lived in as of this moment. He was ashamed to think it, but he couldn't stop himself.

Cody loved James.

James was dead.

And Kai loved Cody.

Kai could finally be honest with himself because the outcome that he never dared to hope for was suddenly possible. A wall that Kai thought he'd never be able to surmount had just been torn down. A tragedy and a miracle had taken place all in one instant.

Still, Kai had to stop himself from celebrating. There was no silver lining for Cody in this moment. She was devastated and needed his support.

"I'm so sorry," he whispered into her ear.

Cody leaned into him, her body still seizing up. Kai looked around at all the Ones from the camp.

"Can you give her some space, please?"

They dispersed, moving farther down the tracks. Kai knew the train would be coming soon. He had to get Cody ready to ride. He couldn't let her disintegrate right where she had stumbled down.

"We'll make them pay for this, Cody," he said. "I promise."

Cody didn't respond.

"But right now we have to get ready to hop on the train."

Cody finally looked up at him and shook her head. "I'm not going back to the Ark."

Kai pulled back from her, his tenuous hopes for this mission and his life suddenly shattering.

"What? Cody, come on. We'll figure it out from there. There's nothing else we can do here." Kai paused for a second. "And besides . . ."

He knew he didn't have to finish that sentence. Cody knew just as well as he did that Edith wanted her back at the Ark immediately. A deal had been made, and Cody needed to fulfill it. As the leader of the mission, Kai was responsible for making that happen.

"Screw Edith Vale," Cody said, her voice shaking. "If she hadn't released the List, none of this would've happened. James would still be alive. You can tell her to go to hell for me."

"Cody. You know that's not true. Now more than ever, we need to get back at them. We need to take out Agent Norton. We need you to tell Edith what you know."

"Tell her I'll handle Norton myself," Cody said. "James saved me from her, but I failed to do the same for him. Now I have to make sure she dies." Cody looked away from Kai, her eyes raging with an anger he hadn't seen from her before.

"That's crazy. Come back, tell Edith the intel, and we'll all make sure it gets done. Together."

"There is no intel!" Cody screamed.

Kai felt his stomach drop. "What?"

Cody stared at him, her body tensed like a caged animal's. "I made it all up! There's nothing to tell!"

Kai staggered back and let go of Cody. He couldn't believe what he was hearing.

"No . . . ," he said, his anger starting to build.

"Yes. And who cares? I wanted to free James and everyone else in that camp. So I lied. What does it matter now?"

"You can't just do that to Edith." Kai was thinking out loud. He knew that Edith would have Cody's ass for making her look so dumb.

"Well, I did. And what does that say about how smart and perfect she is, huh? Maybe you should wake up and realize you don't have to worship her."

Kai had known Edith for long enough; Cody wasn't

going to change his mind about her. Her leadership had been proven to him already, many times over. All he had to remember was the state of their resistance movement before she reached out to him, before she initiated her Locust Project, back when the New Weathermen were merely a gleam in his eye. The only reasons any Ones were fighting now was because of Edith Vale.

But Kai held back from yelling at Cody. Even if she had played him and Edith for fools and betrayed their cause, he still believed in her. In a way, he admired her more for fighting so hard for what she wanted. She was the same girl he'd first heard about in Shasta, who wouldn't back down and swore to fight for justice.

Or maybe he was just lying to himself and forcing himself to believe it. Either way, he knew he couldn't be separated from her right now. He'd felt that certainty when he'd embraced her. Despite her actions, he needed to convince her to come back to the Ark.

And not for nothing, Kai also knew how furious Edith was going to be if Cody didn't return. Not only had Cody embarrassed her, but the essential piece of intelligence she had promised didn't even exist. Edith would go crazy if she didn't get a chance to respond.

It would be dangerous at the Ark for Cody, but Kai already was planning to appeal to Edith's logical side. After tonight, Cody suddenly seemed more motivated and radicalized than ever. Sure, she might not be trustworthy anymore, but if viewed simply as a weapon, she was primed to explode. He'd convince Edith they could exploit that rage. He'd have to.

Kai stood up and brushed himself off. He took a few steps back from Cody, hoping to defuse their fight so he could get through to her.

"Look, Cody, I'll handle Edith and make it right with her. You don't have to be afraid."

"I'm not afraid," Cody said. "I just don't want to go back there. There's only one thing I want now."

Kai waited.

"I'm going to kill Norton," she said. Then she stared directly into his eyes. "Good-bye, Kai."

"Cody, she's a top government official surrounded twenty-four-seven with security. You'll never pull it off."

"Watch me."

"It's not possible alone!" Kai shouted, growing angry.

But Cody was totally calm. "It is if you're willing to die."

Kai knew she was serious. In her mind, her life was already over, and she didn't care how risky it would be to go after Norton. That was all she had left.

As Kai thought desperately for a way to break through that, Taryn walked over.

"It's almost here," she said, gesturing down at the tracks.

Sure enough, Kai could hear the distant rumble of the engine. The train would pass around the curve in about a minute.

He reached his hand out. "Come on, Cody."

She shook her head. But Kai could see that she had lost the crazed look in her eye. The reality of going off on her own must have set in. He looked for what he'd seen atop the quarry, the part of Cody that sensed there was something deeper she and Kai needed to explore together. They still had that chance. Cody couldn't just throw it away all by herself.

The rumble of the train grew louder, echoing off the tree trunks now.

Kai kept reaching out. Only ten feet away, tears formed in Cody's eyes.

"Come with me, Cody. Please."

The headlight of the train emerged from the darkness. The other Ones started jogging along the edge of the track, readying to jump.

Kai knew that in ten seconds he might never see Cody again. After what he had finally admitted to himself, the thought sickened him. Maybe his only chance to stop her was to confess how he felt. Kai considered the pain and humiliation that might result; it was still probably worth it.

Suddenly, it was too late. The engine car moved past them and the tracks were shaking now, their rhythmic clang filling the space between Kai and Cody. It was too loud for even a shout to be heard.

The middle of the train passed, the empty boxcars starting to fill up with Ones leaping on board.

Kai had to decide. He could chase after Cody or return to the Ark. He tried to close the distance, to yell over the train.

"Cody, please—"

But she didn't hear him. She was gone, sprinting like a deer back into the woods. She had decided for him.

Kai didn't have any time to spare. He ran a few steps and leaped for the last train car, his heart so heavy that he barely made it aboard.

＝

Bone-tired and back in his bed at the Ark, Kai couldn't fall asleep. It was the middle of the morning, but all he wanted was to turn his brain off and drift away. The train ride had lasted the better part of the night, and then they had to hike back up through the mountains. Over thirty weary Ones from the camp had made it back with them, making the journey much slower. As for the rest of the kids who had been in the camp, Kai didn't know where they were, but at least he'd given them a chance at freedom.

Of course Edith had been waiting for them when they arrived. It didn't take her long to see that Cody wasn't in their ranks. After she put on a brave face for the new arrivals, she walked past Kai with a look of disgust.

"This whole mission is a failure," she said under her breath.

Kai ran after her, trying to explain what had happened.

It's not like he'd lost track of Cody and squandered the chance at getting her intelligence. There was never any information to begin with. If that was the only thing Edith cared about, then it was, by definition, impossible for the mission to succeed. He could tell Edith was embarrassed. It was true that Cody had outwitted her, and Edith stormed off without another word to Kai.

Now he was staring at the ceiling in his cabin, totally spent, going over the same simple fact again and again in his mind: Cody was gone and she wasn't coming back. Kai felt so stupid. His silly fantasy was impossible. All the moments he'd dreamed of sharing with Cody would never happen. An inside joke that always made them laugh. A kiss that felt warm and scary at the same time. And, if they were lucky, one day standing together, knowing they'd won the fight for the Ones. That they'd dismantled the Equality Act. That Ones could be free.

It was all stolen from him now, even if Kai never really had it. But for a moment by the train tracks, he had let himself believe it. The loss felt real.

Kai knew he needed to stop obsessing over this. Instead, he tried to find a silver lining in Cody's leaving. It was actually pretty easy. The one thing that had stopped him from giving himself over to her was his fear that she would leave someday. Like everyone else had left him. And now Cody had, too.

Better now than later.

The thought made him angry, but also energized. Kai finally gave up on the idea of sleeping. He jumped off his cot, bounded out of the bunkhouse, and began walking with no destination in mind.

The Ark was alive with activity. The new Ones were getting acclimated. Other people kept up their routines, chopping wood, building new structures, tending to the food. Kai's encounter with Edith had made him feel useless. He needed something to do.

Kai's walk led him to the barn, behind Edith's cabin. As he went past, several people emerged from the building—Edith, Ramona, and Taryn. They caught sight of Kai and immediately stopped their conversation. Then they turned and walked in the other direction.

Even more irritated now, Kai looped back to the bunkhouse, and a moment later, Taryn popped in. Without looking at him, she went over to her cot and lay down.

"What was that about?" Kai asked.

"What?"

"You, Edith, and Ramona."

"Nothing. Don't worry about it."

"I'm not worried. I want to know what you were doing in the barn."

"Dude, we haven't slept in forever. Can we drop it for now?"

"Taryn, tell me what's going on," Kai said, his anger creeping into his voice.

Taryn sat up in bed. "I'm sorry if this is awkward, but Edith wants me to lead a special project. She told me not to talk to you about it."

"Why? I already know the whole Ark-as-a-base-camp thing is a cover for its real purpose. I remember all the medical tests she put us through last year. I remember the equipment she was setting up."

"Sounds like you're up to speed, then. I was told not to elaborate, to you or anyone else."

Kai stared at Taryn, seething.

"Look, I don't agree with her; I hope you know that," Taryn said. "But I'm supposed to listen to her, right?"

"Not about this. Not when she's trying to drive a wedge between us."

"That's not what she's doing. Just look at it from her perspective. The last few missions you've been in charge of haven't exactly worked out."

"The fact that they worked out at all is because of me. The lab with the Vaccine got bombed, didn't it? We fought off the Equality Team at the quarry as well as we could, didn't we? And now a whole camp full of captured Ones is free, aren't they?"

"Like I said, don't blame me," Taryn said. "I'm just repeating what I was told, even though I'm not supposed to. I might be the only one left who still has your back."

Kai scoffed. "Really? Then would you mind removing the knife for me?" Taryn didn't seem to find that very funny, and Kai couldn't help from going further. "Why don't you just admit it: You always wanted to outrank me, and now you're jumping at the chance."

"Of course I want to outrank you! Is there something wrong with wanting to be in charge? Or is it only you who's allowed to want that?" Taryn paused and collected herself. "Kai, we've been in the gutter together too many times for me to stab you in the back. I'm just telling you the truth. And the truth is you need to get your act together. I hope that you will. Especially now that she's gone."

"Cody?" Kai hated that Taryn was bringing her into this.

"She took away your edge," Taryn said. "We need it back . . . if you still want to help us."

Kai stood up and stormed out of the bunkhouse. If Edith thought he'd lost his edge, she had another thing coming.

=

"We had a deal."

Kai had planted himself firmly in front of Edith and hissed the words at her. He had barged right into her cabin and found her reading by the fireplace in her spartan living quarters.

"You know what we agreed to a long time ago," he continued. "I'm not going to let you back out of it."

"Kai. Take a seat and calm down. What exactly is bothering you?"

Kai stayed standing. "When you recruited me into the New Weathermen, you made it very clear what I was expected to do."

"And what was that?" Edith said, annoyingly calm.

"You said every movement needed extremists. The wackos. The bogeymen. The lunatics who want to watch the world burn. You said you needed pawns to do the dirty work. If those extremists exist, then by definition there's a more reasonable group to negotiate with. The civilized ones, the house cats. You said if any group wants something bad enough from the people in power, they just need to have their crazies start burning things down. After that, the rest of them will seem a lot more tolerable."

Edith smiled. "You're smart. You understood me."

"Oh, I understood you perfectly. And then I went out and I did it! Exactly like you told me to."

"And look how well it's worked," Edith said. "They're terrified of us. The government has lost its mind. The laws they put in place, the camps, the restrictions—it's all absurd. If we didn't make them panic, if we didn't count on them to overreact, we'd be finished. Who could possibly sympathize with a group of kids born with every advantage? Slowly but surely they would have marginalized us. But a group of kids hauled out of their mothers' arms and dragged away to an internment camp? Now, that's sympathetic." Edith paused. "Congratulations, Kai. *You* caused it to happen."

"Then why are you cutting me out?"

"Everyone has a role in this fight. You've served yours."

"I'm not just cannon fodder. I want to know what's really going on at the Ark. I've earned it."

Edith regarded him for a long time, to the point where Kai started to become uncomfortable. He couldn't guess what she was thinking, but eventually he sensed a feeling from her that almost resembled pride. Finally, she nodded.

"I'm impressed, Kai. You're right, you should know what's going on." She stood up. "Follow me."

Edith opened the door and stepped out of her cabin. She walked the narrow trail over to the barn with Kai trailing behind her. He was almost in a daze over how well the confrontation had gone. He knew that with a simple insistence of "Ones first," Edith could justify any decision or punishment. Several Ones had been unceremoniously kicked out of the Ark with just that terse phrase and a glare from Edith. But Kai had made his case, and she hadn't banished or demeaned him. He'd won her trust, by fighting for it.

At the steel door of the barn, Edith typed a long code into a security box. A pressure valve released with a hiss, and Edith turned the handle. They stepped inside to another door, with a second security box that Edith typed into. The interior door opened, and Edith gestured for Kai to walk forward.

He entered the cavernous room and looked around, astonished.

Edith had a plan all right. And it was beautiful to see.

CHAPTER 7

IT TOOK CODY a full day of hanging around truck stops and begging rides to make her way to Shasta. She used her best judgment in approaching drivers who looked like they wouldn't alert the authorities—or tell her to hop in and try to do something even worse. There was a lot of waiting around and a lot of time to think. She tried to use it to somehow come to terms with James being dead.

Cody couldn't believe it was him and not her who had met such a brutal fate. With all the crazy extremists on both sides of this issue, James was the most even-tempered person she knew. He had been the one who kept preaching calm and understanding, who told Cody they had to keep their heads down while this all blew over. Yet somehow he ended up at the center of the violence, taken away to a camp and singled out to receive the Vaccine, with fatal consequences.

With a pit in her stomach that never seemed to go away, Cody tried to imagine how agonizing it all must have been for him—not physically, but emotionally. After all, his brother Michael had been the one to capture him. And of course his father had helped to create the Vaccine. James's family had always seemed so perfect, and now they'd destroyed themselves. It was a stark reminder for Cody: The debate over how to handle the Ones was *that* powerful.

Cody tried to remember James outside of this whole mess—just the sweet, gentle boy who loved her. Who made her feel special regardless of how she was born. Who always let her have the last french fry. She clutched the scrap of his shirt tightly in her hands and cried for what felt like the hundredth time. The spot where James had written *PQ3318* was smudged with dirt, but the message was clear enough for Cody: James was thinking about her right until the end.

But Cody hadn't made it in time. She'd failed him. Now her thoughts had to turn to how she could honor James. It wasn't by sitting around and waiting at the Ark, that was for sure. Cody knew there was only one thing left to do: kill Agent Norton, the person responsible for causing all this pain.

It wasn't just because of what she'd done to James.

Norton also had it coming for everything she'd done to Cody during the unbearable weeks Norton had held her in captivity. The isolation and deprivation. The waterboarding and suffocation. The insistence, day after day, that her life was over—that she was a terrorist with no rights and no hope. Cody would gladly wipe Norton off the earth for all of that, but James's death gave her determination a new, overwhelming urgency. It was all Cody could think about.

Killing Norton wouldn't be easy, Cody knew. She was a high-level government agent, probably surrounded by an extensive security detail. And Cody had no guaranteed way to locate her, let alone get close to her. These were legit obstacles, but Cody wasn't worried. She had her personal brand of stubbornness on her side, and she knew she'd find a way eventually.

She also knew attacking Agent Norton would very likely lead to her own death. Or indefinite capture and detention, which felt like the same thing. That was why she wanted to make one last trip through Shasta: to say good-bye to her mom.

The last time Cody had run off to join the fight, she'd left her mother with only a note. In the days that had passed since, she'd come to regret leaving like that. Maybe it was coming so close to actually dying. Maybe it was having a little more time to process who she really was. Or maybe it was just the simple desire to have an honest conversation—and at least one last hug—from someone who truly loved her. After all that had happened, that sounded truly comforting. Almost miraculous.

When Cody's last ride pulled into Shasta, she jumped out at a gas station in the center of town. It was a short walk to her old neighborhood, but Cody took her time. A lot of memories rushed to the surface, and Cody almost had to laugh. She'd been gone only a matter of days, but the memories felt like they were from a different lifetime.

Of course that had been a different time, before the Equality Act had taken effect. Persecution against Ones was the law of the land now, with a formal set of regulations targeting the genetically engineered. As Cody scanned the familiar landscape, Shasta and its people appeared the same, but she felt the difference. It wasn't just the Equality flags and offensive bumper stickers—those had always existed, just like there would always be moronic bullies at the high school, trying to pick fights.

No, what Cody sensed now in her hometown was a bleak feeling of acceptance—acceptance that the traditional standards of society people had previously striven for were simply too hard to maintain. Respect, compromise, and decency seemed impossible now. In their place, a mob mentality of fear, anger, and selfishness had come to the fore, modeled shamelessly by the highest figures in government. Of course Cody thought there was only one side to blame for this, but she also knew her attitude just perpetuated the problem. It was a vicious cycle, and as Cody walked around, Shasta seemed consumed by it.

When she made it to her street, Cody's disappointment faded away and a wave of excitement fell over her. She walked to her front door, speeding up when she saw the light from the television, an old nature documentary probably, bouncing around inside the small house. Cody tried the door handle, but it was locked. She knocked softly.

After a moment, the door cracked open and her mom's face appeared. A shout of joy rang out. The door flew open and Cody's mom leaped forward, hugging her so hard that Cody staggered backward. But her mom held on, and they fell over together on the scraggly front yard. Her mom's tears turned to laughs of joy as she held Cody down and began kissing her cheeks. At this point, Cody had to consider her own safety, so she raised her arms to protect herself.

"Mom, you're crushing me!"

"Oh, stop, you deserve it, Cody! I thought I'd never see you again!"

"Can you let me off the ground, please?"

Joanne stole one more kiss, then helped Cody up. There was still a giant smile fixed on her tear-streaked face.

"Now get your butt in the house, young lady."

=

Cody spared her mom the worst of the details, but she told her most of what she'd endured since slipping out of the house. There was the bombing, the funeral for James's dad, the fight against the Equality Team at the quarry, the escape through the forest fire. She didn't reveal anything specific about the Ark, but she told her mom about the raid on the camp and that James was dead. Her mom joined her in crying for him all over again. She had loved James, too.

Joanne had been following the news reports about the camps, but she didn't know things were that bad. Everything that reached her through the media was sugarcoated just enough to seem reasonable. The government bulletins and statements made it sound like they were simply dealing with a crisis, not descending into unadulterated totalitarianism. Her mom's discouraging recap hardened Cody even further. Finally, as she was wolfing down a homemade omelet, Cody broke her own uncomfortable news.

"I'm leaving again, Mom," she said. "As soon as possible. Tonight."

"Cody, don't even talk like that! You're not going—"

"I'm serious. I've already decided. I just came to say good-bye. Properly, this time. Please don't fight with me while I'm here."

"After everything you just told me? Cody, it's not safe out there! You can't keep taking risks like that. I will lock you in your bedroom if I have to."

Cody stood up and backed away from her mom. She

needed to let her know that physically trying to stop her was not going to fly.

Her mom tried a gentler tack. "Cody, you've been through a lot, you're traumatized. Ever since they took you away, I know it's been hard. You need help, you need stability, not more chaos. You have to trust me."

"I'm fine. My head is fine."

Joanne started crying. "You'll get yourself killed. And for what? Look at you, you have so much to live for, so many possibilities."

"*Possibilities?*" Cody shot back. "Do you see what's going on out there?"

"You don't have to get sucked into it anymore. You can do whatever you want."

"I want to avenge James. That's all I care about now."

"More violence?" Joanne yelled, aghast. "You know that won't solve anything."

"It will. For me."

"And what about me?"

"That's why I came to say good-bye."

Her mom stared at her. Finally, Joanne said it, something she'd clearly been holding back. "It's an insult to me if you throw your life away so young. I gave up everything for you, devoted my whole life to giving you a better chance. I didn't do it so you could toss it away at seventeen in some kind of noble tantrum. You have the chance to do so much more, to truly change the world." Joanne paused. "And if you waste that, if you rush out of here and get yourself killed, you might as well be spitting in my face."

Joanne turned away from Cody and went to the sink. She wasn't going to watch if her daughter really left like this.

Cody's heart broke for her mom, and she understood the truth in her statement. But there was something else her mom had left out.

"You want me to do something with my life, right? Make my mark, leave an imprint? Well, I'm not going to wait around and hope that happens one day. I have a chance *right now*." Cody stepped toward her mom, willing her to turn around. "The people who took me away, the people who killed James, the people terrorizing all the other Ones—I can't let them get away with it. Someone needs to show the world this isn't acceptable, that they will suffer the consequences. If I'm the person who does it, that's a worthwhile life, no matter how long it lasts. *That* will be my mark on the world."

Cody paused and took her mother's hand. She continued, softer now.

"And, Mom—if I manage to do that, then it *will* validate what you did. The choice you made for me, all the sacrifices, it will all be worth it. It will be your contribution to the world just as much as mine."

Cody held tight to her mom's hand and watched

Joanne's head bow forward, tears tumbling down. They stood there for a long moment, mother and daughter, sharing a whole lifetime together in a wordless embrace. And then, at last, Cody pulled her hand away.

"I love you, Mom."

=

After leaving the house, Cody didn't have much of a plan about where to go. She considered heading back to the truck stop to catch a ride out of town, but to what destination? Washington, D.C., where Norton worked? Maybe that's where she should head off to, but it seemed impossibly far away. For the time being, Cody figured she could spend the night at the quarry, in the mining tunnels where the Ones had made their camp. Hopefully there was a stray sleeping bag and some canned food left up there.

As Cody began the long hike up into the foothills, she found herself on the street where James had lived. Maybe it was only muscle memory that brought her in that direction, a reflex from hundreds of previous jogs, but there she was standing across the street, staring at James's old bedroom window.

It was dark, of course.

Fighting the urge to go closer, Cody stood still, remembering all the times she'd met James right in this exact spot in the street. She had the urge to tell him about her plan for Norton and almost started talking out loud. Then she thought of everything else she wanted to tell James. Perhaps she'd be doing this for the rest of her life. Cody must have spaced out for a while because suddenly, without her seeing anyone, a voice called out.

"Cody?"

She squinted into the shadows beside the house. Someone was approaching her. Just as Cody was about to spring away, she saw the person's face.

It was Michael, James's older brother.

Cody immediately started to back away. She didn't know what he wanted, but Michael was volatile and dangerous. And the last time she'd seen him, he was apprehending James at gunpoint.

"You can relax," Michael said as he walked closer. "I'm not going to tie you up or anything."

Kind of hard to believe, Cody thought. She stayed primed to run.

"If you're here on a nostalgia tour, I guess you already know what happened," he said.

Cody had never liked Michael, had never felt any sympathy for his situation. So what if his younger brother was a One? Michael was also born with every advantage. He was a winner of the genetic lottery, too, the old-fashioned one, and he could have been a little more gracious about it. Now the way he was talking about James dying—it was just a reminder that he was a horrible person.

Still, she nodded at him. "Yeah, I heard."

"All right, then," Michael said with a sigh. He turned and walked to his front door. "Might as well come inside."

Cody was shocked that he was inviting her into the house. Had Michael forgotten everything? They were enemies even before the violence broke out between the Ones and the Equality Movement. And now they were literally fighting for different sides. But Cody realized that as of a few days ago they shared one inescapable bond: James was dead. Maybe that trumped everything else.

She decided to follow him into the house.

It was dark and quiet. Michael hit a light switch to reveal that it was messy, too.

"My mom is staying with her sister. My dad . . . and James . . . well, you know . . ."

Cody considered again the fate that had befallen this family. They had always seemed like the paradigm of the American Dream, but that image had turned out to be a facade. And now it was irrevocably shattered, Cody realized. She wandered through the darkened house, a place where she had never really been comfortable, but now it felt even weirder. She kept expecting to turn a corner and find James sprawled out on a couch. She could almost feel him, but he never appeared.

In the dining room, Cody found Michael seated at the large table. They had argued there or exchanged dirty looks too many times to count. But as soon as Cody entered, Michael began speaking in a rush, as if he was desperate for someone to talk to.

"I found out from the Equality Team I volunteered with. They are still around here getting help from some of the local militias, and they told me what happened." Michael lowered his head, tearing up. "That's not what I wanted for him."

Cody could tell Michael was a wreck. He certainly looked it. Still, she was in no mood to be sympathetic. "Then why did you help bring him in?" she asked.

"He let our dad get killed! How could he do that?"

"Your dad was making the Vaccine."

"He also saved you, remember?" Michael shot back. "He got you out of a place that no one comes back from."

Cody nodded. It was a fair point—and the reason she had tried to save their father from the bombing.

"And he wasn't going to give the Vaccine to James," Michael continued. "He told us that. He was trying to make a safe version for everyone."

"A 'safe' vaccine to change all the Ones? Come on, Michael, listen to yourself. That's not possible."

"Well, they still weren't supposed to kill him!" Michael wailed, then really broke down. "Why'd they do that to him? Why?"

Cody was silent for a minute. She gingerly stepped closer to Michael and took a seat at the table.

"So you're angry at them, too?" she asked cautiously.

"Of course I am. Forget about James, I never thought that any Ones should be *killed*. I'm not a monster."

"Okay. We agree about something, I guess," Cody said. "I'm actually going to do something about it, though. I'm going to kill Agent Norton, who *is* a monster."

Michael looked up at her. "Agent Norton?"

"She's in charge of the Equality Task Force. She's the one who authorizes all this stuff. Who put the target on James at the camp. And now I'm heading to D.C. to nail her."

"I know who she is," Michael said. "And that's your plan? Just walk up and shoot her? It's never going to work; you won't even get near her."

There was the old condescending Michael she knew, the bitter older brother who couldn't accept anyone outshining him. But what bothered Cody even more was that he was probably right. It wasn't much of a plan.

"I'll figure it out," she responded defiantly.

Michael let the matter rest for a moment, and Cody was grateful he didn't want to revert to their familiar fight. But then he asked her a question. "You really think Agent Norton is responsible for my brother's death?"

"I know she is. I've met her. I know what she's capable of."

Cody could see wheels turning in Michael's head. Clearly sitting around alone in this bleak house thinking about his brother had begun to wear on him. Maybe this was the moment he'd been waiting for, but Cody didn't know what to expect.

Michael finally looked up at her. "What if I could get you near Agent Norton?"

Cody jolted upright. "You can do that?"

"If I could . . . ?"

"Then I'd avenge your brother. I'd kill her, for James." Cody paused and leaned forward. "Michael, are you willing to help me do that?"

Michael stared back at her, the guilt in his eyes giving way to smoldering anger.

CHAPTER 8

WHEN KAI WOKE up the next morning, he was still thinking about what he had seen in the barn the night before. It was thrilling and creepy at the same time—and it reminded him of the stakes of their fight. Ever since Cody had refused to come back to the Ark, he'd been trying to convince himself there were more important things to focus on. He needed to see Edith's secret to remember why he'd invested so much time and energy in the New Weathermen—to remember that he was committed to shaping a world where Ones were truly free. The contents of the barn had proved they were readying one major step toward that goal.

Edith had also planted a different seed in Kai's head. Afterward, as they walked to his bunkhouse together, she'd said, "Remember what we agreed on in my cabin: We have to win their sympathy. The mob, the mainstream—we have to change their minds."

"Yeah, I understand," Kai said.

"That means doing things we don't like sometimes. Things that are hard for us in the moment."

"Edith, what are you trying to tell me?"

Kai had felt uncomfortable as Edith spoke to him. He wished she wasn't always so cryptic.

"Talk to Taryn," she said, patting him on the shoulder. "I put her in charge of a new mission."

Having slept on it, Kai still felt uneasy about this exchange. He knew Taryn was already angling for more responsibility at the Ark. That meant she'd agree to anything Edith asked.

Kai caught up with her at breakfast. As a bunch of groggy Ones moved down the food line, Kai gestured to Taryn. They filled their plates, stepped outside, and found some stumps to sit on.

"Edith told me to ask you about something. The new mission . . . ?" Kai tried to conceal his apprehension.

"She did?" Taryn seemed surprised. "That's weird—she didn't tell me to loop you in."

"Well, now she wants you to," Kai said. Then, after a moment, "Unless you think I'm making it up."

Taryn stared at him for a second. "No. Of course not."

"So what is it, then? The new mission."

Taryn looked around, then dragged her stump closer to

Kai. She seemed pretty tense. Finally, she leaned in to him. "We need to kill a One."

What did she just say? Kai didn't understand. He made that clear to Taryn from the look on his face.

"A One is going to get killed," she said. "A false flag attack. We do it ourselves and make it look like a horrible hate crime. It'll be so ugly that people will have no choice but to feel bad for us."

"So we stage a murder? And make it seem like the Equality maniacs did it?"

"Exactly. Except someone really has to die. And it has to be a real One."

"James is already dead," Kai said. "Let's expose that. Isn't that enough?"

"That was done behind closed doors," Taryn said. "They can make up whatever story they want. Our job, if we can pull it off, is to leave behind a mess that they can't possibly explain away."

Kai grasped the basic idea, but he still couldn't believe they were considering this. Even after everything he had signed up for, it still made him uncomfortable. If he had a line he wouldn't cross, this was it. He knew it might help them to win sympathy from a portion of the more moderate population—but would that justify killing an innocent kid?

He posed that question to Taryn.

"It might," she responded. "If it saves the lives of hundreds of others. Thousands, even."

"There's no way to know that," he said.

"If there was, would you agree to it?"

Kai sat on his stump and considered it. Of course he would trade the life of a single One to save a multitude of others. But something about handpicking the unlucky victim changed the equation. As much as he supported radical tactics in order to win this war, to actually choose someone to murder felt unconscionable. And conscience aside, he had to admit it also irritated him that Edith had asked Taryn to lead this mission and not him. He would have refused, but it still stung. Maybe Edith really meant it when she said he'd already served his purpose.

"I don't know, Taryn," he said.

"You don't have to know. That's why I'm running this one."

"That doesn't mean I'm going to let you . . . "

Kai suddenly trailed off as he saw Taryn fixate on something over his shoulder, her eyes narrowing with anger.

"Well, this is just great," she snarled.

Kai turned around to follow her gaze and then promptly dropped his bowl of oatmeal. He couldn't believe his eyes.

Cody was walking into camp.

And striding right alongside her was James's asshole brother, the gun-toting volunteer for the Equality Team who had chased them through the woods like criminals and betrayed his own blood.

Kai didn't know whether to run and embrace Cody or duck behind a tree and start shooting. After a moment, it was clear from their body language that they hadn't come to attack the Ark. As they made their way out of the woods, the rest of the Ones poured out of the mess hall to stare menacingly at the new arrivals.

Kai and Taryn pushed to the front of the crowd. As they passed Cooper, Taryn said to him, "Some security we have up here. People can just wander in at will?"

"Don't look at me," Cooper said, irritated. "Our security is that we're in the middle of nowhere, and no one is supposed to know about us. You were the ones who showed her how to get here."

By now Cody and Michael had followed the trail to stop right in front of Kai and Taryn.

"I took your advice and came back," Cody said to Kai with a grin. "Just ended up taking me a little longer."

Kai tried to suppress his excitement at seeing her again. He knew she had an ulterior motive—why else would Michael be with her?—but he couldn't help hoping he was part of why she'd come back. Maybe he had written Cody off too soon. Just when he was starting to forget about her and rechannel his energy into the Ones, she strolled into camp like she owned the place. It would have been a lot cooler, though, if she hadn't brought a travel buddy.

Kai felt the tension in the crowd of Ones behind him. He forced himself to look stern as he gestured at Michael. "What the hell is he doing here?"

"Don't worry," Cody said. "He's here to help."

"Help drag us off to a camp?" Taryn said.

Michael, keeping a step back from the group, shook his head solemnly. "I wish I had never done that."

Suddenly Edith emerged. Her eyes fell on Cody and immediately inflamed with rage. She parted the crowd of Ones and walked straight up to her. Edith's arm shot out and grabbed Cody by the throat.

Kai and Michael jumped in to try to pull Cody and Edith apart. Cody flailed in shock and gasped for air, and Kai took one look at her reddening face and managed to tear Edith off her.

Edith pushed him away, stepped back, and gathered her composure, keeping her gaze on Cody the whole time. "You're not welcome here anymore. Leave now, before we kill you."

Cody stood still, struggling to recover but waving Michael off, and Kai noticed something new in her: an odd measure of calm. For some reason, she wasn't scared. In fact, she was almost smiling.

"I thought we had a deal?" she finally said to Edith.

"We did," Edith said. "You broke it. Now go."

"I promised to give you intel about Agent Norton." Cody nodded at Michael. "Here it is."

"It's too late to keep lying," Edith said. "Kai already told me you were bluffing, that you didn't have anything to trade." Edith pulled out a gun. "I'm serious. Get moving."

Kai knew she wasn't messing around. Cody had humiliated Edith, and now she'd brought a member of the Equality Movement to the Ark as well. Horrified, he realized Edith might not even let them leave alive. They had seen too much now. She could be planning to simply shoot Cody and Michael as soon as they turned around.

Edith raised her gun.

"Kai told you I was bluffing?" Cody asked, shooting him a look. "Kai doesn't know everything, I guess." She pulled Michael forward. "This is Michael, James's brother. And he's going to help us kill Norton."

Even as Kai felt the sting of Cody's disappointment in him, his spirits were lifted by her confidence. Maybe she hadn't been totally honest with him, and she did have a plan all along.

Edith seemed torn. "I'm not falling for any more empty promises."

Kai jumped in. "Why would she come all the way back here just to lie? It wouldn't make any sense."

"I'm not lying, Edith," Cody said. "If you want the intel, you can get it just by lowering the gun."

Edith moved the gun away from their faces, but Kai could tell she wasn't convinced. He leaned in to Edith's ear.

"I know you'll never fully trust her," he whispered. "But I promise you this girl wants Norton's head on a stick. Turn her into a weapon. If she succeeds, great . . . and if she fails, you won't lose any sleep."

Edith stood expressionless as she listened to Kai. After a tense moment, she locked eyes with Cody. "You really have a way to get Norton?"

Cody flicked her eyes at Michael.

"I know the schedule for when she visits the camps," Michael said. "A buddy of mine on the Equality Team— sorry, a guy I knew—explained it to me. I know all the protocols: what day she'll be at each one, what time she arrives, when she leaves, how she travels. I know exactly how we can hit her."

"And why would you tell us all that?" Edith asked suspiciously.

Michael lowered his eyes. "For my brother James."

Edith pondered all of this for a moment.

"Edith, you've always wanted Norton," Kai said softly. "This is the best edge we've ever had on her. You can be responsible for finally taking her out."

Kai could feel the energy of the other Ones shifting. They had come outside ready to pounce on Cody, but now they were licking their chops for the chance to actually take down Agent Norton, a tormentor who had taken on a mythic significance to them all. Kai stared at Edith, willing her to give Cody this chance.

But Edith, of course, was never one to be manipulated by the power of the mob. She pointed at Cody and Michael. "Tie them up and lock them in the woodshed," she said to Cooper, then walked back calmly into the mess hall to finish her breakfast.

=

A little later, after the crowd had dispersed and everyone had moved along to start their day, Kai made his way to the woodshed. The flimsy door was barred from the outside, and Cooper leaned against the wall next to it, a gun slung over his shoulder.

"We're not holding any visitors' hours," Cooper said. "Edith made that clear to me."

Kai held up his hands and stopped thirty feet short of the shed and simply stared at it. Cody had taken a gigantic risk by coming back to the Ark, and now she was locked up like a prisoner. It didn't sit right with Kai.

He heard footsteps and wheeled around to find Taryn approaching. He realized they hadn't finished their argument from earlier that morning.

"A little jumpy, huh?" she said, then gestured toward the shed. "Don't even think about it."

"Think about what?"

"Doing something crazy so you and Cody can run off together, maybe try to kill Norton on your own."

"Why not?" he asked. "I thought her plan sounded pretty good. We should all be up for it."

"Kai, I'm serious," Taryn said. "Please don't mess this up for me. I'm about to lead our new mission, and it's important. As a friend—please."

"That mission is insane," Kai said bluntly, staring at Taryn. It didn't feel right being on a different side from her, but he truly believed that Cody's plan for Norton made more sense for them. They'd be killing an adversary, not an innocent.

"Edith approved it," Taryn said. "Take it up with her."

"You know what? We should." Kai started walking away. "Let's go."

Taryn chased after him. "Damn it, Kai, I didn't mean literally."

But he was already bounding across the Ark toward Edith's cabin. Taryn had no choice but to follow, and a few moments later Kai was knocking on Edith's door.

An angry voice from inside asked, "What is it?"

"Can we come in? It's me and Taryn," Kai said. "We need to talk." They waited outside with no answer, until finally Edith opened the door and let them inside. They all stood in the small, dark interior.

As Edith glared at them, Kai laid his cards out. "I don't get it, Edith. If we want to fight back against the Equality Movement, we have to target Norton. Why are you wasting this opportunity?"

"I agree with you," Edith said. "That's why I decided to go ahead with the plan to take her out."

Kai was confused. "You did? Then why'd you lock Cody and Michael in the woodshed?"

"So that girl can think long and hard about screwing me over again," Edith said with a measure of satisfaction. "Gets pretty hot in there, don't you think?"

Kai shook his head. He didn't know whether to be grateful that Edith was on board to go after Norton or freaked out about how she was tormenting Cody.

Taryn, on the other hand, was clearly anxious about what this meant for her. "So we leave them in there for a week or two, do the false flag mission, then shift our attention back to Norton?"

"A week or two?" Kai yelled. "Are you nuts?"

"Not exactly," Edith said to Taryn.

"Edith, you told me this mission was a priority," Taryn said. "You told me I could lead it. I want to move as soon as possible."

"This thing with Norton is time-sensitive," Kai said. "Who knows when she might switch up her routine? False flag can be carried out whenever."

As Taryn seethed, Edith nodded. "The Norton mission is actually a great companion to your directive, Taryn. But it has to go first. Once we take down Norton, it will make a lot more sense that an innocent One was targeted and killed. The public loves a compelling narrative, and this will play out perfectly for them."

"This is bullshit," Taryn said.

Kai watched as Edith's eyes narrowed and filled with menace. "Are you questioning my decision?" she asked. "Is it not enough for me to simply tell you this way is better? Is it not enough to know that I always put Ones first? Is it not enough to remember that without me setting this all in motion, you'd be a helpless, squiggling larva stuck in the mud?"

Taryn was legitimately tough, but Kai could still see the fear rising within her. As Edith stared her down, Taryn finally nodded. "No, of course I trust your decision," she said.

"All right, then," Edith said, calming down. "You heard me—let's go get Norton." Then she stared directly at Kai. "But I still don't trust that sneaky little friend of yours. Which means neither of you is leading this mission."

"Then who is?" Kai asked, his voice trailing off as the answer slowly dawned on him.

Edith couldn't hide her grin. "I am."

CHAPTER 9

THE SUN HADN'T come up yet, but Cody was wide awake and starving. She was sitting at a picnic table at a highway rest stop in West Texas, somewhere in the hill country between El Paso and Marfa.

The vast night sky and wide-open expanse was a far cry from the time she'd spent cooped up in the Ark's woodshed. That had been pretty annoying, but Cody had obviously experienced much worse. She and Michael had slept through an uncomfortable night before Edith opened the door and informed them that she had approved their plan. A day later, they were on the road, heading south.

Now, on the Texas roadside, Cody locked her attention on Kai as he walked out of the gas station with a box of doughnuts. There was a lot to do that day, but at the moment, she was just really hungry.

Kai put the box on the table and stepped back as Cody, Michael, and Taryn dug in with abandon. Of course Edith was there, too, but she didn't take a doughnut. Cody almost had to laugh at the absurdity of this breakfast club. If someone had told her a few weeks ago that she'd be eating at a Texas gas station with this cast of characters, she would have refused to believe it.

Michael had been dead to her. Now he was the linchpin to achieving her ultimate goal. And somehow, she actually had faith that he was being sincere.

Edith Vale had been an enigma who was responsible, in Cody's eyes, for provoking all the recent mayhem. Now she was an accomplice and the leader of the Ones' fight. Or at least it seemed that way—Cody still wasn't fully sold on Edith's wisdom and virtues.

And Kai—well, Cody couldn't really figure out how she felt about Kai, then or now. She did know, however, that she couldn't stop thinking about their moment together at the top of the quarry.

To be sure, it had occurred during a very unique and brief window in her life: James had said he wanted nothing to do with her anymore, and she also thought she was about to die. Was that the only reason she had connected with Kai right then? The moment was too fleeting to provide a clear answer. A second later James returned and saved her. It was hard to explain it in hindsight.

Still, she couldn't deny one firm element of truth: Thinking back on it made her heart race every time.

Cody looked over at Kai as he licked powdered sugar off his fingers. Now was not the time to figure it all out. They were about to kill Agent Norton.

It had been a whirlwind couple of days focused on planning and logistics. After getting them out of the woodshed and debriefing Michael, Edith had led them down from the Ark on a different path than Cody was used to. The trail eventually led to an old mountain road where they piled into a dented Land Rover that was concealed in the woods. They drove south for a whole day and night before reaching Texas. In the car, Michael repeated what he knew about Agent Norton's routine. Thankfully, his contact on the Shasta Equality Team had previously worked on her security detail.

Every Friday, Norton dropped in on one of the internment camps built for the Ones. The camps, several dozen of them, were sprinkled around the country, each holding hundreds of kids between the ages of six and twenty. They were intentionally set up away from population centers, not entirely inaccessible but well off the beaten path.

On each trip, Norton traveled by private jet to the nearest army base. She would then proceed in a motorcade of three cars to the camp. The vehicles were modified Cadillac Escalades, with tinted windows and bulletproof glass. Norton rode in the backseat of the middle car. This week, she was scheduled to visit the camp built for the southwestern section of the country. And the Weathermen planned to be there on Friday morning.

They spent Wednesday morning scouting Route 17, the one-lane highway that led to the camp. It ran through and curled around low hills of brush and chaparral. Unfortunately, there was no cover from any trees, but the rolling topography meant you couldn't see very far into the distance. Eventually they found a place to lay their trap.

All of Thursday was spent buying vehicles in El Paso. Edith and Michael had to handle this, leaving the suspicious-looking teenagers behind. They scooped up two old pickup trucks, a rusted repairman's van, a flatbed logging truck, and a motorcycle for Kai. That was all for the assault. And then two of the most boring, nondescript cars possible for their getaway. As each newly acquired car came into the fold, Cody felt like a parking valet, driving them around to where they needed to be positioned.

As for the cost, it seemed to Cody that Edith had access to a deep well of money. Cody had no clue where it came from, and she couldn't help feeling a little bitter. Her mom could never afford to buy Cody even the crummiest old car, and yet here they were, collecting them by the bushel.

Now it was Friday morning, and they were all ready to disperse from their staging area. The crew looked exhausted, but Cody could see everyone catching their second wind, the significance of their mission finally setting in. Edith stood up from the picnic table, a clear indication it was time to get moving. She didn't need to bother with any kind of pep talk.

"See you on the road," she said.

Cody jumped behind the wheel of the van, and Edith took the passenger seat. They had ripped out the back seats so they could toss Norton in when they apprehended her. Cody would have preferred killing her on the spot, but Edith had convinced everyone it might be worthwhile to keep Norton alive for a few minutes.

As Taryn and Michael walked to their respective pickup trucks, Michael passed by Cody's window and leaned in quickly.

"Thank you for coming back and finding me," he said.

"No problem," she responded. "Thank you for not sneaking out of the shadows and killing me that night."

"James would get a hell of a kick seeing us try to pull this off, don't you think?"

"This would be his nightmare," Cody said, laughing. "We're about to break like fifty laws and a dozen basic safety rules."

"Well, let's not rile him up too bad. Stay safe out there."

Michael gave her a quick fist bump, moved to his truck,

and drove off. A moment later, Kai peeled out in the other direction on his bike. Inside the van, Cody adjusted her seat and mirrors so that everything was perfect. Next to her, Edith set up a mobile command station around the front seat with maps, a police scanner, and a walkie-talkie.

They were ready.

Ready, it turned out, to wait.

=

Four hours later, Cody, Edith, and their van hadn't moved. It had been a long morning of tense silence. And Cody had finished a family-size bag of Swedish fish.

They were on lookout duty, facing the road from the rest stop parking lot. Finally, as the sun started to really sizzle, a line of Escalades raced past them. Cody nudged Edith with excitement.

Edith clicked her radio. "Cobra just drove by position one. Prepare position two in ten minutes."

Cody buckled up and reached out to turn the van's ignition, but Edith grabbed her arm and made her wait a few moments longer. When she finally nodded, Cody pulled out onto the road. They followed behind the motorcade from a safe distance, far enough that Cody could barely see the SUVs ahead of them. But they knew where the turnoff was to get to the camp. After several miles, Cody reached it and turned the van onto an empty, lonely country road. Somewhere in the hills ahead of them, Norton's motorcade was heading for the rest of their crew.

As they went deeper into the rugged backcountry, Cody sped up a little. It was important to be on the scene immediately after the assault went down. As Cody rounded a bend, she saw the brake lights of the SUVs ahead. They were all screeching to a stop, trying to avoid a flatbed truck that had been left blocking the road. Cody smiled. The speed bump had worked.

The Escalades came to a halt in front of the truck. Maybe they were considering driving around it, but the off-road terrain was pretty dicey. This moment of indecision was all the Weathermen needed.

In an instant, a pickup truck came blasting out of the hills and rammed horizontally into the first SUV. The two vehicles careened off the road in a cloud of dust.

Just as quickly, another pickup truck raced out of the hills from the other side of the road and smashed into the trailing SUV. As metal cratered and tires squealed, black smoke poured forth from the tangled cars.

A single Escalade remained in the road. Norton's car. And now she was a sitting duck. From a few hundred yards away, Cody gunned the van toward her.

Before she got there, Kai had raced up on his motorcycle from the other direction. He rode right up to the front bumper of the final Escalade. Then he took out a gun and pointed it directly at the windshield.

On the other side of the car, Cody and Edith had pulled

up to the scene from behind, ready to grab Norton if she made a run for it.

For an impossibly long moment, no one moved. The only sound came from the wheezing engine of one of the totaled trucks. Cody tried to peer into the SUV to see Norton. She had to know she was trapped.

There was no surrender, though. Instead, the SUV revved its engine and charged forward at Kai. He fired several shots into the windshield, to no avail. At the last second, he dove out of the way as the car knocked away his bike and almost crushed him against the flatbed truck that had been left to block the road. Then the SUV reversed course and raced backward, slamming into Cody's van.

The jolt sent Cody's adrenaline surging. She was ready to crush whoever was in that car. But the maneuvering had created a small window for the Escalade to turn sideways. It bolted off the road, around the flatbed, into the weeds, and then veered back onto the open asphalt. Suddenly, it had clear sailing.

"Go, go, go!" Edith shouted.

With the two pickup trucks crashed and Kai separated from his bike, suddenly the van was the only chase vehicle. Cody twisted the wheel, turned off the road, and gunned the van past the flatbed. They bounced jarringly over the scraggly earth until Cody got back on the road. Far ahead, the Escalade was racing away from them. Cody stomped on the accelerator and took off after it. No way in hell she was going to let Norton get away.

They started flying down the narrow road, and the sloping hills turned the ride into a roller coaster. At some turns they lost sight of the SUV as it rounded a bend, but Cody never slowed down, even as the van's tires wailed on the frequent curves.

"We have to catch up with her before she reaches the camp," Edith said. "That's not much time."

"I'm going as fast as I can!" Cody yelled.

The reckless driving began to pay off; she was cutting the distance between the two cars. As they got closer and closer, Cody glanced at Edith. "What now?"

"You have to ram them."

Cody nodded. She could do that, gladly. Just a little closer.

She was almost on the Escalade's tail, ready to bump it when something flashed in her side mirror. Kai was on his bike, racing up from behind her, then zooming past.

Ahead of the van now, he caught up to the SUV. As Cody and Edith watched, Kai took out his gun and in one fluid motion fired shots into the front and back tires on the SUV's left side. The vehicle immediately popped into a somersault and tumbled over its front bumper, then rolled several times, finally stopping in a ditch on the side of the road as a cloud of dust rained down.

Cody slammed on the brakes, and their van stopped just beyond the wrecked SUV. Kai also screeched to a halt. He hopped off his bike and ran toward Norton's vehicle, gun leveled. Cody and Edith got out and joined him, circling the flipped-over SUV.

The wheels spun in the air, but no sounds came from the car. Cody knelt down and peered inside. She caught sight of the driver and quickly turned away before she was sick.

He was definitely dead.

Behind him was Agent Norton, hanging upside down from her seat belt in the back seat. As Norton blinked at her through the dust and the blood trickling down her face, Cody saw the moment of recognition.

Damn, did that feel good.

There wasn't time to gloat, though. They cut the seat belt and dragged a dazed Norton through the window. Kai held her down and disarmed her while Cody went back to the van for the zip ties, blindfold, and tape. They got Norton secured in the back of the van, then Kai jumped in with her while Cody and Edith got in front. Within a minute, Cody had them turned around and headed in the opposite direction. She glanced in the rearview mirror to catch Kai's eye. They both grinned with pride.

Edith raised her radio to her mouth. "Heading back to position two. Cobra is in her cage. Be ready to jump in."

Cody drove back to the scene of the motorcade assault.

As the van arrived, Taryn and Michael stepped out from behind the wrecked cars. Kai opened the back door and they jumped in.

Edith turned to Cody. "Position three, as quickly as possible."

As Cody drove, Edith turned her attention to the police scanner in her lap. Already there was a constant stream of chatter about their operation. Norton or her driver must have called it in during the chase.

Cody got back to Route 17 and then quickly abandoned it for a maze of side roads. They finally pulled off onto a dead-end street dotted with crumbling trailer homes. The two getaway cars were waiting at the end of the road. Everyone jumped out and prepared for the switch.

As Cody watched Edith lead Norton to the cars, she felt a pit in her stomach. "We're going to kill her here, right?" she asked.

Edith kept going to the car and opened the back door. "Let's get moving. We'll talk about it later."

Cody looked to Kai, who didn't meet her eyes. "Hey!" she yelled. "You said we were going to kill her!"

Edith shoved Norton into the car and walked back to Cody. "She's worth more to us alive than she is dead. We can interrogate her, use her as propaganda, use her as a bargaining chip."

Cody was incredulous. "You mean let her go eventually?"

"No. I mean play it smart. Remember what we're after here, Cody. We want to overturn the Equality Act. Keeping her alive could be essential to that," Edith said.

Cody couldn't believe it.

This wasn't going to help James, or make her feel any better about having been tortured, or make it up to all the Ones who had been persecuted, rounded up, and altered. And more important, Norton hadn't earned any mercy or a stay of execution. She was still the woman who had yanked the bag over Cody's head and smiled as she suffocated. She was still the woman who had singled out James for an injection that left him dead. That's all Cody could see looking at her now—death, pain, and misery.

Cody knew it in her bones: Norton had to die.

Without another word, she walked up to Kai, snatched the gun out of his waistband, then darted to the car and opened the door. Norton, bound and gagged, cowered in the back seat as Cody pointed the gun at her.

"Cody, stop!" Edith yelled.

But Cody knew what she had to do and knew that she was capable of it. She had dreamed of this moment in her cell countless times, and now it was even more justified. She pressed her finger to the trigger.

"Cody, wait! Just listen to me."

That was Kai's voice. She couldn't help but glance over. He pleaded with his eyes, but Cody forced herself to look away.

"Think about James, Cody!"

And that was Michael's voice. She turned toward him now, shocked he wasn't on her side. "James would want what's best for the Ones. Not just him. Put the gun down."

Cody shook her head, trying to tune everyone out and keep her focus as she felt her heartbeat pound between her temples. The rage felt like it was going to crack her skull wide open. She needed to let it out. She turned back to the terrified Norton.

"Cody, please!" Kai yelled. "Just wait one second. I won't stop you after that. Just let me ask you one question."

Cody's hand began to tremble as she kept it level with Norton's head. "What?" she finally yelled in exasperation, her whole body shaking now.

Kai took a step forward and lowered his voice. "Who do you care about more right now, James or all the other Ones? The Ones who are stuck hiding or in camps or in danger. The Ones who are five years old and can't go to school. Who do you care about helping? Who can you *actually* help?" He paused. "However you answer, I promise I won't hold it against you. But please, think about it for one second."

On the quiet dead-end street, everyone stood still, waiting to see what Cody would do.

She switched her gaze from Kai to Norton and back again. The sight of Norton cowering in the car filled her with disgust and rage. But Kai's words made her feel something she'd almost forgotten. They reminded her of a person and a place in time that Cody felt like she couldn't access anymore, a mirage just beyond her reach. Too much had happened to her and too much had changed. But even with all that distance, she recognized something familiar in his question. It was a question she must have asked herself before: Are you going to live for yourself, or are you going to live for others?

In this moment, with her hand wrapped tightly around the gun, she so badly wanted both. But she knew that was impossible. She had to choose.

CHAPTER 10

EVERYONE WAS SILENT, their nerves rattled, as Edith drove the getaway car out of the dead end. From the back seat, Kai stared at Cody, who was riding shotgun. Even if he'd known what to say to her, he could tell she didn't want to hear it. Not from him, not from anyone.

Kai turned to his left. There was Agent Norton in the back seat next to him, tied up, blindfolded . . . and alive.

The standoff at the car swap was over. Cody had ultimately listened to him, but it had cost them precious minutes—when they should have been getting away from the area as quickly as possible. Edith had the police scanner turned on, and the activity was frantic. The authorities had found the demolished SUVs, the dead agents in the security detail, and of course they'd discovered that Norton was gone. An all-out search was under way.

Edith steered the car north, in the direction of the Ark, desperately hoping to get on an interstate highway filled with thousands of other cars. As the police chattered over the radio about where they were setting up checkpoints, Cody dutifully marked them on the map. A few miles ahead, Michael and Taryn were in a scout car. They would call back if they saw any trouble.

Kai strained his eyes trying to look out ahead of them. He knew too much time had gone by since they'd attacked the motorcade. The bulk of it was wasted trying to prevent Cody from killing Norton, and now their window for escape was closing. He grasped for the gun Cody had reluctantly returned to him, knowing he might still need it. If they got stopped by the authorities or tried to outrun them, the last part of their plan was obvious: They'd have to kill Norton, after all.

Suddenly, that seemed like a real possibility. Edith's walkie-talkie crackled, with Taryn on the other end. "Checkpoint ahead, mile marker sixty-three on Route 17. Do not proceed here."

Edith slowed the car and picked up the radio. "Copy."

Norton, perhaps thinking they were close to being spotted, started thrashing around. Kai leaned across the back seat, pressed Norton's head against the window, and whispered in her ear.

"Move another muscle and I am going to start breaking your fingers one by one." He paused. "Got it?"

Norton sat still as a statue.

Kai stuck his head into the front seat. "What do we do about the checkpoint?"

"We need to get off the roads," Edith said. "We're not making it through their dragnet today."

Kai felt the extra pressure of Edith being on this mission with them. She hadn't left the safety of the Ark in a long time, so to expose herself like this was very rare. Kai could see that she was feeling the pressure, too.

Leaning forward, Edith scanned the hilly countryside, and Kai followed her gaze. Not a lot of places to hide, and not much civilization to blend into. And off in the distance a group of helicopters had started to dot the sky like a kettle of vultures.

Cody, engrossed in the map, jolted up. "Look here!" she said, pointing. "There's a lake we can get to on the back roads. It says there are some campgrounds next to it."

Kai and Edith leaned in to check it out. They could certainly get to the lake. And holing up at a campground was definitely less suspicious than driving around with Norton in the car.

Edith nodded. "Navigate for me."

The tires squealed as she spun the car around.

=

Lakeview Luxury Cabins was a bit of a misnomer. A more fitting name might have been Pond-Adjacent Plywood Shacks. But Kai and the others were in no mood to complain about false advertising. They had all made it safely and undetected into one of the stand-alone cabins, and that was good enough for now.

With Cody calling out directions, Edith had driven them toward the lake without encountering a checkpoint. She'd dropped off Kai, Cody, and Agent Norton about a mile away from the campground. Norton wasn't too big of a problem—she was securely tied up, and Kai just had to drag her around like a piece of luggage. They disappeared into the hills and waited for nightfall, then snuck into the cabin Edith had rented. Taryn and Michael joined them shortly thereafter.

The shoddy cabin had a small bedroom, a living area, and lots of surfaces covered in fake wooden siding. It was tight quarters for the five of them and their hostage, but for the moment it appeared they were safe. No one was suspicious of the polite, solitary woman who had rented the cabin. As long as they kept quiet and out of sight, they could probably head back to the Ark undetected in a day or two.

As he poked around their new hideout, Kai could already tell how boring it was going to be. There were a few romance novels in the cabin and a deck with forty-six cards. At least that was enough to toss into a hat. He anticipated getting really good at that.

Stepping into the kitchen area, Kai opened the fridge. Empty, of course. They'd have to cope with the meager snacks they had in the cars. He turned around to find Edith had come over to stand right next to him.

"Kai," she started, leaning in so no one else could hear. "Hell of a job today. I'm proud of you."

Kai tried to conceal his smile. And before he could even respond, Edith walked away.

In the spirit of team unity, Kai knew he also had a post-mission message to deliver. He found Michael across the cabin and tapped him on the shoulder.

"Hey, thanks for the intel today. I wasn't sure we could trust you, but, I gotta say, it all checked out."

Kai was never going to be interested in a friendship with Michael, but he could at least drop his outward disdain. They wouldn't have Norton in custody without him.

Michael nodded back at Kai. "Yup, no hard feelings. I'm glad we got her."

With that settled, Kai walked away. He'd made his point, and now he joined everyone else in finding a comfortable spot to sprawl out. The whole crew was exhausted, of course, but they couldn't all crash at once. Someone always needed to be on guard duty with Norton. Someone other than Cody, Kai figured. Edith volunteered to take the first shift.

"You guys get some sleep," she said. "I'll wake someone up in two hours."

Then she dragged a reluctant Norton into the bedroom.

Kai and the others watched from the doorway as Edith shoved her into a narrow closet. Edith lifted the blindfold from Norton's head, and their eyes met.

"This is real. This is actually happening," Edith said, making sure she had Norton's full attention. "Now I need you to think about whether you want to be a problem or a solution."

Norton tried to speak, but her mouth was taped up.

"Take your time," Edith said as she slammed the closet door. She placed a chair firmly against it, sat down, and leaned her head back. She nodded for the others to leave the bedroom.

Out in the living area, the rest of them stretched out on the furniture or threw pillows on the floor to lie down on. Kai hit the lights and found a spot on the carpet near Cody, across the room from Taryn and Michael. He was physically drained, but there was no chance he'd be able to fall asleep. Taryn and Michael, on the other hand, were quickly snoring on the two couches. Kai looked over at Cody, wondering if she was as wired as he was. He saw her tossing and turning.

"Crazy day, huh?" he whispered.

She propped herself up and registered Kai was sitting next to her. She quickly wiped her eyes.

"You all right?" Kai asked. She didn't respond. "I know it was hard for you to make that decision today. But you made the right choice."

"It's not that. It's just . . ."

Cody trailed off, and even in the darkness Kai could see tears stream down her face.

"Tell me, Cody."

"I just have this really weird feeling. I can't really explain it."

Kai didn't want to alarm her, but he sensed it, too. "Yeah, that was crazy back at the car swap. I've never seen you like that."

"Me neither. It's scary."

"Well, let's forget about it now. You didn't go through with it. It's over. You're going to be fine."

Kai had aimed to be reassuring, but his hopes were dashed as Cody suddenly stifled a loud sob.

"I don't know who I am anymore," she said. "I'm not a One, I know that. But I don't feel like a normal person, either."

When Kai nodded, Cody raced on. "James is dead. There's nothing left for me in Shasta. So I felt like killing Norton was the only way—the only thing left for me to do. And that's not a real identity, just wanting someone dead. So now what do I do? Where do I go? Who am I now?"

As Cody looked at him desperately, Kai took a deep breath. He knew she felt like she was going crazy, but these question weren't crazy to him.

"I get it," he said softly. "I've never been sure about

my identity, either. And I mean that literally—like, I really don't know who my parents are, where I'm from, what my heritage is. And I understand that weird limbo, of only kind of feeling like a One. I know that technically I am, but for a lot of my life I didn't feel like it. Ones aren't usually kicked to the curb and passed around foster families like an old rug. They don't usually have to scrap and claw just to survive. They don't have to—"

Kai stopped. He felt himself getting angry, and that wasn't what he wanted. "Anyway, I'm just saying that I understand that feeling. You're not alone in being confused sometimes. And I have nowhere to go after this, either. Whenever 'this' ends. Maybe that's why it's so important to me."

Kai saw from Cody's expression that she appreciated what he was saying. It was a nice reminder for him, too, about what had drawn him to Cody in the first place. She was another person whose life wasn't simple, another person with a lot of gifts and a burning desire to use them. And now, someone else who was realizing there was no guidebook for exactly how to do that.

"That's why I wanted to kill Norton so badly today," Cody said. "If we don't know what happens next, it would have been nice to at least do that one thing. Win that one fight."

"Whatever comes next, it'll be better for us to have her alive."

"You really think we can use her to change anything?" Cody asked, sounding unconvinced.

Kai couldn't fill Cody in on their next mission, but he wanted to at least assure her that some good would come from sparing Norton's life. "I do. If we get her back to the Ark and play our cards right."

Cody shook her head. "I don't buy it. There will just be another version of Agent Norton we have to deal with tomorrow, and then another the next day. And the people who agree with these policies, the Equality Movement, you can't reason with them, they'll always hate the Ones. It's all pointless. There's no future for us here."

"Stop that. A small group of really crazy people can always change the world," Kai said.

"They can also be squashed down by the government and never heard from again." Pure sorrow made Cody's voice waver. "We're not winning, Kai. They are."

For the first time, Kai fully understood how low Cody was. It had been a whirlwind few months for her and she had suffered and lost a lot. She also had a valid point; judging by the most obvious metrics, the Equality Movement was a glorious success. The Supreme Court had banned any new genetic engineering. The laws in the Equality Act had transformed the Ones into second-class citizens. Now they had been branded dangerous enough to ship off to internment camps. In short, the concept that they were less deserving of their rights had been utterly normalized. And all too soon, if the Vaccine was effective, there wouldn't be any Ones left. Kai could see why Cody was so disillusioned.

Which is why he had to tell her about what he saw a few days earlier in the barn. He needed her to understand that all wasn't lost.

"Cody, there's something you should know," he started tentatively. "Things aren't as bleak as they seem."

"What do you mean?"

"At the Ark, there are measures we are taking to make sure the Ones never disappear. To create a world where being special won't have a stigma. Where Ones can be free."

Cody stared at him. "You mean in the barn?"

Kai nodded. He saw a glimmer of excitement flicker in her eyes.

"Kai, tell me what you're talking about."

He reached out and took her hand. She didn't pull it away. She squeezed it.

"I can't tell you everything," Kai said. "But just know that there will be a future for us. I promise."

Kai stared back at her, hoping he had killed her cynicism, but also hoping for so much more. Suddenly this cramped cabin with their snoring comrades across the room felt like the most romantic place in the world.

"A future for . . . us?" Cody asked softly, holding his gaze.

The question sent a jolt of excitement through his body. But Kai was still nervous.

"Us," he replied firmly.

And then he no longer had a choice, or even control of his body.

He leaned forward and met Cody's lips in a kiss so perfect it made him forget that anyone else had ever existed.

CHAPTER 11

CODY COULDN'T GET her heart to stop racing. She was lying next to Kai on the floor of the cabin, the exhilaration of their kiss still leaving her light-headed. Cody remembered when he first whispered in her ear at the diner in Shasta; even then, she craved a closer connection with his energy. That was why she could never take her eyes off Kai. It was also why she grew scared anytime they got close to each other—she knew she wanted to get closer, and that one day she wouldn't be able to help herself.

Everything Cody was afraid of had just been proven true, but in a good way. Kissing Kai was electric. Pressing her body against his sent fireworks off in her brain. Their embrace had lasted for less than a minute—they were entangled on the floor in a room full of people, and they'd both pulled away from each other before that became awkward—but Cody knew she wanted more. For the time being, she had to settle for lying beside Kai, knowing he, like her, was wide awake and staring at the ceiling. Cody reached out and slipped her hand into his.

But as her exhilaration waned, Cody was overwhelmed by confusion. Was she betraying James's memory by even admitting this attraction for Kai? Should she embrace it, or bury it like she had been doing? What did she owe to James?

She still loved James, of course. But James was dead; being in love with him wasn't even possible anymore. Still, Cody felt like there was a waiting period that she was violating. Maybe she owed James more time, somehow. But the reality of the moment she'd just shared with Kai proved her body had other ideas. Maybe Cody needed to have a little more faith in herself: She could grieve for James and fall for Kai at the same time.

Her heart was big enough for that.

Putting aside their kiss for a moment—actually, that was no fun, so Cody closed her eyes and relived it again. She squeezed Kai's hand and edged closer to his body, hoping he was still thinking about it, too.

Okay, putting it aside now, Cody was touched by how Kai had finally opened up to her about his past. Unlike James or anyone else she knew, he truly could relate to her experience. In their own unique ways, they were both Ones, but not Ones. They were both fighters who had dealt with rejection. She had always sensed a dark origin to Kai's anger, and now she understood it.

And Kai had just reminded her of something even more important: Sometimes you can lose sight of what else you have to live for. Cody had been in a spiral of disillusionment about what was left for her in this world. Suddenly, as of a few minutes ago, she couldn't wait to discover her next day. There would be another kiss, deeper understanding, new energy. Kai would be involved, and that felt worth racing toward.

Cody must have been lying awake with her butterflies for quite a while, because eventually she heard Edith come into the living room.

"Is anyone awake?" Edith whispered. "Who wants the next shift?"

Cody practically leaped to her feet.

"I'll do it," she said. She couldn't sleep anyway; might as well do her part.

Edith looked at her with an amused smile. "Yeah, right."

"What's wrong? I'm the only person awake right now."

"Yeah, and you're the only one liable to kill Norton if we leave you alone with her," Edith said. "No chance I'm letting you watch her."

"Look, I understand now—it makes more sense to keep her alive. I can handle it."

Edith simply shook her head and walked right past Cody. She reached down to the closest body on the couch, gently shaking Michael awake. He looked up at her groggily.

"Time for your guard duty," Edith told him.

Michael nodded and slowly stood up, then lumbered into the bedroom. Edith took his place on the couch, ignoring Cody's angry glare.

Between the jolt from the kiss and now the insult from Edith, Cody was even further from sleep. She spent at least an hour squirming around on the uncomfortable floor. Finally, growing stir crazy, she got up and poked her head into the bedroom. At least she'd be able to talk with the other person who was being forced to stay awake.

When she got into the bedroom, Cody found Michael slumped over in his chair, completely asleep. She walked over and prodded him.

"Michael . . . wake up. You have to stay awake in here."

Michael mumbled something and barely moved.

"What's up with Norton?" Cody asked, looking at the closed closet door.

No response. Clearly his shift on guard duty wasn't going to work out.

"Michael, want me to take over for you? You can go back out there and lie down."

Somehow Michael seemed to understand this, because he stood up and staggered to the doorway.

"Thanks," he managed to mumble as he left the bedroom.

Cody was alone now, staring at the closet that held Norton. She placed her hand against the cheap wooden door, softly to avoid making a sound. It felt good to be the captor this time.

Eventually, Cody sat down, her chair pressed against the door. She could hear Norton shifting behind her. She had come in here to think about Kai, but Cody couldn't help herself—immediately her thoughts turned to the weeks of torture she'd endured at the hands of the woman who was now inches away. The drowning, the misery, the hopelessness. The total disregard given to her as a human being. It all came flooding back to Cody, triggering the rage she'd just recently brought under control.

Cody knew there was no use trying to fight it now. She and Agent Norton needed a reckoning.

So she stood up and opened the closet door.

A blindfolded Norton lifted her head, sensing some-one standing above her. It gave Cody a shameless sensa-tion of joy to see her so helpless. She let Norton thrash about for a moment, then reached down and lifted the blindfold.

Norton stared back up at her, and Cody saw the fear creep into her eyes. With no one present to stop Cody, Norton thought it was her time to die.

"Not yet," Cody said softly. She wanted to make sure no one heard her in the other room. "But you know you deserve it, right?"

Norton tried to talk through her tape, but it only came out garbled.

"How small does a person have to be to do what you did to me?" Cody asked. "How heartless, how pathetic, how afraid do you have to be to do that? Are you disgusted by yourself? Or do you try not to think about it?" Cody paused. "I'm not sure how much longer you're going to be alive, but I hope you use every minute to remember how big a piece of shit you are."

And Cody couldn't help herself. She didn't plan on it and she wasn't proud of it, but she knelt down to Norton's level and spit directly in her face. Really, it was the least she could do.

Norton recoiled, ducking back into the recesses of the closet. Cody smiled, remembering her desperate attempts to find safe haven in the corner of her own cell. A small measure of payback had been cashed in.

Cody stepped away, ready to shut the closet door again, but Norton edged back into the doorway and tried to talk again. Cody couldn't understand a word, of course, but she was actually curious to hear Norton's defense. Weirder, though, was Norton's frantic eye movement—glancing to the living room and back, and then nodding her head. It seemed like she was desperately trying to indicate something.

Knowing full well it was a mistake, Cody just couldn't resist. She pulled the tape off Norton's mouth.

"Listen to me very closely," Norton started, softly and breathlessly. "We need to move quickly if this is going to work."

Cody was stupefied. Did Norton actually think Cody was going to help her? She snorted in disbelief.

"Cody, you have to trust me now," Norton whispered. "We need to get out of here."

Cody laughed. "How dumb do you think I am? You're not going anywhere. The rest of your miserable life is going to be spent tied up in a cage. Now shut up and get used to it."

She started to shut the closet door, but at the last second, Norton called out, "Do you want to see James again?"

Cody froze. She jerked the door back open and stared down at Norton. In spite of all her instincts, that question had gotten her attention. Norton still knew how to push her buttons.

"What are you talking about?" Cody asked warily. "James is dead."

"No, he's not. And I can help you get him back. But we need to leave here right now, you and me, together."

Cody tried to keep her composure. She reminded herself to think rationally. Find out the truth.

"He's dead," Cody said. "They told me. They saw him."

"No one claimed they actually saw his body, did they?"

Cody tried to remember exactly what she'd heard from the other Ones at the camp.

"Of course no one saw it," Norton continued, "because I saw him alive just the other day." She paused before delivering the kicker. "If we get out of here, you can make a trade. Me for him. Now how does that sound?"

It sounded crazy. It sounded like a trick, like another one of the manipulative psychological ploys that Norton had tried on Cody during her detention. But it also sounded just a little bit . . . possible?

"Come on, Cody, you know this is an amazing opportunity. One hostage for another. Get me to a phone and I can arrange everything."

"I need proof," Cody said. "How do I know he's really alive?"

"You have to trust me. You know how badly I wanted to get Edith Vale. Well, James was the best lead I had. I planned to use him to get Kai, and then use Kai to get Edith. I needed James for that. When I heard he was captured, I immediately had him transferred to my custody. Whatever they did to him at the camp was only to get the other kids to fall in line."

"That's a great story. But it's not proof."

"How I can prove it like this?" Norton held up her bound hands. And Cody knew they'd already destroyed her phone so it couldn't be used to track her. "Just listen, all right? I was questioning him two days ago—"

"You mean torturing him."

Norton sighed. "Interrogating him, okay? He told me

156

about the first Weathermen meeting you guys went to, in the church basement, when he tracked you down. Isn't that right? How else would I know that?"

Cody tried to think if there was another way for Norton to learn that. It sounded like it came from James. But even if she knew how rough the questioning could be, she didn't love the fact that James was spilling his guts.

Norton went on. "And he told me what happened there. The girl who pulled a gun on him, the head of security, Monica. Isn't that what happened?"

Who the hell is Monica? And then Cody realized— James may have talked, but he had tried not to include any details that could actually hurt the Ones. *That's more like it*, she thought with pride. Even without the correct details, though, Norton's story made sense. She might actually have heard that version of events from a living, breathing James.

"Even if you did question him at some point," Cody said, "that doesn't mean he's still alive."

Norton shook her head in disappointment. "Cody, come on. We would never kill him. That's just brutal and against the law. We want his intel, but we're not monsters."

Cody begged to differ, obviously. But she had to concede that if James was seen as a potential link to stopping the Weathermen, it wouldn't benefit anyone to kill him. It was impossible to know for sure, but Norton's story, as disturbing and self-serving as it appeared, actually made sense. Cody felt a sudden, bright hope that James really was still alive.

But even if he was, could she trade Norton for him? Betray Kai and Edith and the rest of the Ones just for James?

Norton kept laying it on. "Cody, you know me pretty well, I think. You may not like me, but you know I don't lie. I've always been straight with you. Now let's just leave, and I promise to make this deal happen."

"I don't need to run off with you right this second to get James back," Cody said. "Edith wants to negotiate a bigger deal, one that involves repealing the Equality Act. Now that you told me he's alive, I can make sure he's included in that."

"Edith doesn't care about James! Come on, you know she has her own agenda. And I'm guessing you're not totally in on it, either."

Cody considered this for a second. It was true that Edith didn't have much of a track record for putting individuals over the group.

"But, Cody," Norton continued, "forget that for a minute and think about this: Now that I've been kidnapped, what's James's life going to be like in the meantime? Put yourself in his shoes—I know you can. My colleagues think he might have information that can be used to find me. They are talking to him right this second, I'm sure. *Interrogating him.* How's that going to play out?"

Cody's stomach heaved at the thought of what was surely happening to James. He was getting pressed for information he didn't even have. Norton was right—Cody did know how that went. And she couldn't allow it to happen. She'd never be able to live with herself.

Even more pressing was the obligation she felt to do whatever it took to save James. He had done that once for her, at the quarry. Even before that, he was the one who got her out of government captivity. That action had come at a tremendous price for him—it had destroyed his relationship with his father, and then it had been part of what got his father killed. James had sacrificed all that for her.

No matter the risks, she knew she had to return the favor. She had to try, if there was any chance he was still alive. And if Norton was lying, well, then Cody could just take her knife and slit Norton's throat at the last second. Cody might not get away after that, but her original goal would still be accomplished.

Apparently Norton could see her mind being made up. "Come on, Cody, do you want to save him or not? We have to do this now!"

Cody locked eyes with Norton, deliberating for one final second. It was a devil's bargain, but she had to take it. She nodded her head at Norton, ready to take the leap.

Norton gestured to her legs, and Cody bent down and cut through her ankle ties so she could walk. Then Norton offered out her bound wrists, but Cody shook her head—keeping Norton somewhat immobilized was fine. She helped Norton to her feet, and they moved toward the bedroom door.

Cody stuck her head out and scanned the living room. Everyone seemed to still be asleep. She saw two sets of car keys on the table by the front door. Yes, this was a savvy crew of revolutionaries, but their guard was down at the moment. Cody gestured to Norton, and they began to move to the door as gingerly as possible.

Passing Edith on the couch, Cody already dreaded dealing with her reaction, should she ever see it. Stealing the biggest bargaining chip away from the Weathermen was not going to be looked upon kindly. But hadn't Kai just told her that some project at the Ark was going to ensure the Ones would be fine? Edith's plans wouldn't all be ruined without Norton.

Cody looked at Kai now, sleeping soundly on the floor, and she stopped.

The news about James had almost made her forget what had happened earlier that night. Seeing him now, his angular face at peace in the shadows, Cody had half a mind to abort the plan. The thought of exploring a future with him had rejuvenated her, and now she was abandoning it just as she began to understand what was possible between her and Kai. She couldn't deny that feeling had made her giddy. But if James was alive, her heart was still spoken for. She had to push her feelings for Kai back inside herself. She tiptoed quietly past him.

They made it to the door, and Cody grabbed the car keys. There was a little jangle, and Cody saw Edith roll over on the couch. She and Norton both froze, but no one woke up. With a few more soft steps, they were out the door and in the middle of the campground.

Being truly in the middle of nowhere, it was almost too dark to see outside. But Cody made out their getaway cars parked near the dirt road, and she ran over to them with Norton. Trying the keys, Cody got one of the cars unlocked and jumped behind the wheel. She threw open the other door for Norton. With a last look toward the cabin, Cody started the car and slowly pulled away without revving the engine. She had to hope no one heard them.

A minute later they were far enough away for Cody to speed up. No one was following. With a few more turns, there would be no way for Edith to find them. Cody stared ahead, determined to find a phone for Norton to use and then a safe place to make the trade. She started to feel confident that James was truly alive. In all the stress of making this decision, she hadn't given herself a chance to celebrate that incredible news. It was probably a good choice; knowing Norton, it was too early to celebrate.

Cody turned to take a good look at her new traveling companion in the passenger seat. Though it was hardly necessary, she reminded herself not to relax around

Norton. As it was, she felt like they were playing out an all-too-literal version of the old folktale where the scorpion asked the frog for help crossing a river, and the frog reluctantly agreed.

Cody remembered all too well what happened once the scorpion got her ride.

CHAPTER 12

KAI WAS DRIFTING blissfully in his favorite place in the world: that weird, semiconscious state of sleep just before waking up. Even though he knew he was still dreaming, he had no control over his mind and how it wandered. Right now, Kai's mind had only one thing floating around—his kiss with Cody.

As he relived it over and over in his fuzzy dreamworld, Kai luxuriated in the feeling of the night before. It was a sensation that could only exist when pent-up nervousness was replaced with overwhelming excitement. The contrast in emotion was so stark, it felt like a state of shock. Warm, fuzzy, elated shock.

"Kai!"

Kai's dream with Cody hit a speed bump, but he fought

hard to stay in it. Compared to the kiss, perfect as it was, the look on Cody's face had meant even more.

"Kai! Get up!"

Kai felt himself losing his dream. He tried desperately to hold on to the feel of Cody's skin under his fingertips—

A hand shook him violently. He woke up in a flash of panic, with Taryn kneeling over him.

"Kai, wake up!" Taryn yelled in his face. It was quite possibly the most unpleasant alarm clock in the world.

He rubbed his eyes and sat up. Edith and Michael were rushing around the cabin. Taryn was dragging him to his feet. He looked around; no Cody.

"What's going on?" he finally managed.

"She's gone," Taryn said.

"Cody?" Kai asked, his confusion growing.

"No, Agent Norton!" Taryn shouted. "And yeah, Cody, too," she added begrudgingly.

"I don't understand—"

"They're both gone. One of the cars is gone. They ditched us."

Edith walked out of the bedroom and came over to him.

"When did you see her last?" she asked.

"Last night, obviously. You were on guard duty. She was lying right next to me when I fell asleep," Kai said. "Who took the next shift?"

Edith and Taryn glared at Michael.

"I told you already, I didn't see anything," Michael said. "I must have fallen asleep in there. I'm sorry. The next thing I remember was waking up on this couch ten minutes ago."

Taryn, enraged, reached for the nearest thing to peg at Michael's head. It ended up being the deck of cards, all forty-six of them. As Kai watched them bounce off Michael's face, he suspected that wasn't quite the effect that Taryn intended.

She pointed her finger at Michael. "I'm going to kill her, then I'm going to kill you."

"Hey, I've got nothing to do with this!" Michael responded.

"Then why'd you let Cody take your shift guarding Norton?" Taryn asked.

"I don't even remember doing that."

"Don't remember?" Taryn asked. "Then maybe you remember the plan you made with them." Suddenly, she pulled a gun out and leveled it at Michael's head. "Seriously, dude, why don't you tell us what you're really doing here?"

Michael tried to back away, only to bump into a wall. "Hey. Please, just take it easy."

"I'm not gonna take it easy when we just kidnapped the head of the Equality Task Force and then had her walk right out the fucking door!" Taryn bellowed, waving the gun around.

Edith stepped between them. "Taryn, enough," she said calmly.

She reached out to take the gun from Taryn, who waited a moment before reluctantly handing it over. Kai breathed a sigh of relief. He'd truly thought Taryn was going to shoot Michael. Not that he would've objected too strongly just a few days ago, but Kai had to concede that the only reason they were able to grab Norton in the first place was because of Michael's contributions.

Edith turned and looked at Michael. "Besides, why would he help us capture her only to let her go?"

"Because of his brother," Taryn said. "He probably wants Norton dead and knows that Cody will actually do it."

"Yes, that is certainly possible," Edith replied.

Kai realized that Edith hadn't put away the gun. In fact, it looked like she was adjusting something on it.

"Wait, that's not true. I—" Michael started to say.

POP

POP

POP

Three bullets in his chest cut him off. Already dead on his feet, Michael fell to the floor in a heap.

Edith turned to Taryn and gestured out the windows. "You were going to use it without the silencer," she said. "That would have been foolish." She handed back the gun.

Kai, in shock, found himself pressed back against the wall. He had to wonder if he was still dreaming; Edith's actions had been so effortless, and Michael had gone down so easily, it didn't feel real. But now Michael was dead and Kai saw that Edith didn't even care. As he stared down at the body, crumpled on the floor, blood already pooling, Kai couldn't believe that Edith had just played judge, jury, and executioner like that. He knew she was ruthless, but not that ice cold.

"He could have been telling the truth," Kai finally said.

"Oh, stop it," Edith said. "He's an Equality Movement bigot. So he got sad about his brother, who cares? These people don't change."

She bent down and lifted one of Michael's lifeless arms. Then she pulled his shirtsleeve down his forearm so Kai could see what was beneath it. The dark, simple tattoo made Kai's skin crawl; it was an equal sign, the stark symbol of the Equality Movement.

"You still want to complain?" Edith asked.

Kai stayed silent. He did, however, want to prevent this same fate from happening to Cody. After last night, Kai refused to believe she would take off with Norton intentionally. Something else must have happened.

"Maybe it wasn't Cody who took Norton away," he said.

"What are you talking about?" Taryn replied.

"Who's to say it wasn't Norton who kidnapped Cody? She got the drop on her somehow and needed a hostage."

"We would have heard something," Edith said. "There

was no fight, no struggle, and the leg ties are cut off cleanly. I'm sorry, Kai—Cody knew exactly what she was doing."

"Then Norton must have made her do it."

"*Made* her do it?"

Kai couldn't believe the alternative. "I promise you, there is no way Cody would take off—"

"Kai, enough already!" Edith startled him by raising her voice. "She's gone. She took Norton and she's going to kill her, probably already has. And if she has half a brain—which I'm not sure about anymore—she's not coming back."

Kai could only hang his head. There was no use arguing with Edith and Taryn; they were already convinced.

"What did I tell you about her?" Taryn asked.

Kai didn't answer.

"You should have listened."

Kai had to wonder if Taryn was right—maybe he should have listened to her about Cody. It hurt to admit, but he could have just been played. Or even more likely, if no less heartbreaking, maybe his connection with Cody had been real, but wasn't meant to last. He would always swear by the moment they'd shared the previous night—but Kai knew special connections like that never lasted. He'd learned it the hard way, the easy way, and every way in between. That's what had held him back from opening up to Cody sooner, and now he was abandoned again. She'd already disappeared and come back once. Kai put himself out there even more this time, and still she had left—and humiliated him. *Fool me twice*, he thought, *then shame on me*.

Now Kai turned his attention to salvaging himself in Edith's eyes. He was responsible for Cody's transgression; he had vouched for her again and again. It was time to simply clean up her mess.

"I'm going after them," he said. "Maybe I can find them and bring Norton back to the Ark."

"Kai, stop it," Edith said. "You'll never find them. And we need to get back to the Ark as soon as possible. Without Norton tied up in the back seat, we can get through the checkpoints." She turned to Taryn. "We've wasted a lot of time out here. Let's get that other mission going right away."

Taryn nodded.

Kai grimaced. He knew what they were referring to, and he didn't have any interest in going back to the Ark to help out with it. He understood there was no avoiding violence in this fight, but Kai didn't want to kill unnecessarily, or to kill his fellow Ones. He glanced uneasily at Michael's body on the floor—none of this met his definition of a justified kill.

"Go back without me," he said. "I'll stay behind and look for them."

"I said no, Kai," Edith said. "We're all going back."

Kai shook his head. He knew it was a long shot to get

Norton back, but he still wanted to go after Cody. He had to see her again.

Edith sighed, clearly frustrated. After staring at him for a moment, she opened the front door and gestured for Kai to come outside. "Take a walk with me, will you?"

Kai felt worried by her tone, but he followed Edith outside. She led him on a walk down to the lake. Kai began to wonder if he was safe with her; after seeing Edith kill Michael like that, it felt like a fair concern.

"I know you might want to quit right now," Edith began, "but we still need you, Kai. All of us."

"I didn't say anything about quitting. You saw what I did yesterday."

"Sorry," Edith said. "I'm not questioning your capabilities. I mean that you're losing focus. On what's important."

"I haven't—"

"So let me fill you in on something you should know. I think it might help kill all these other distractions. Because let's face it, Kai, you've been distracted."

Kai wasn't loving the lecture. But it seemed simple enough to play along. "All right," he said. "What should I know?"

"Remember what I showed you in the barn last week?"

Of course he did. It was a startling and inspiring sight. Dozens of fertilized embryos stored beautifully under their special lights. Each embryo a future peer of his, genetically engineered from the sperm and eggs of Ones like Kai. They would be the next generation of human perfection, and Edith Vale had worked painstakingly to see this vision through. She referred to these embryos as her second swarm of locusts.

Kai was honored to be a part of it. He knew the babies would grow up as the healthiest generation that ever existed, bringing the world closer and closer to a future without any suffering. And even better, when they were born, these babies wouldn't be in the system. The government wouldn't know about them and wouldn't be able to track them. Kai assumed that Edith had a plan to slip them into the rest of the population so they would never get harassed like the Ones.

"I know I told you that the new locusts hadn't been born yet."

"Yeah . . ."

"Well, I left out one thing." Edith paused. "Those embryos you saw won't be the first to arrive. We tested one already, gave life to the first ever second-generation One. And guess what?"

Kai stared at Edith.

"You're a dad."

=

The drive back to the Ark was long and awkward. They had piled into the remaining getaway car early in the morning and pointed it north with a general feeling of fatigue, hunger, and defeat. With her prime scapegoats now either dead or in the wind, Taryn turned her irritation to Kai. She made it clear he had to sit in the back.

Kai spent the ride trying to wrap his mind around the fact that he was suddenly a father. He'd had a vague sense that this was possible when he was at the Ark the previous year. Edith had been obsessed with doing every test and taking every sample imaginable from the Ones there. He didn't know what the purpose was, but Kai knew Edith was planning something ambitious. And now there was a baby that he had helped create. Not by choice or traditional means, but still—it was enough to bring him back to the Ark.

As Kai thought about it more, his anger began to build. What right did Edith have to do this? He supported her grand plans, as far as he understood them, but that wasn't permission for her to order up some offspring based on his genes. Kai knew too well what could happen to babies that weren't planned or wanted, and now Edith had created one from his genetic material. What if she was just starting this nasty cycle all over again?

And how exactly did Edith think this baby and all the other embryos in the barn were going to be integrated into society without major problems? He hoped it wasn't as simple as dropping them off in a cute basket at some random fire station. Yeah, that would ensure the babies survived, but to enjoy what kind of life? Bouncing around the foster care system could be very hard on everyone involved, and it was certainly not an effective tool to solve the equality problem. Kai's experience was a unique exception, not a model to be imitated.

As he stewed, it occurred to him that Edith's plans might actually be *too* ambitious. Between the news about his child and the mission she had approved for Taryn, he began to wonder if Edith's absolute authority was actually good for the Ones. Past experiences had validated her leadership—the existence of the New Weathermen, for starters—but Kai saw that the unchecked power was getting dangerous. As they drove back toward the Ark, Kai stared at the back of Edith's head, a seed of doubt growing for the first time.

At last, after a full day on the road and a final hike through the mountains, they trudged up to the Ark on heavy legs just after nightfall. As they walked into camp, Edith turned to him.

"Do you want to go over now?"

Kai's anger about Edith's unilateral decision to make him a parent didn't mean he wasn't curious. He nodded.

"Follow me."

They proceeded past Edith's cabin, past the barn, and deeper into the woods. The trail disappeared; Kai had never been back this way before. Finally they broke through the trees into a little clearing. There was a small cabin in the middle, by itself.

Edith walked up to the door and punched in a security

code. She pushed it open, and they stepped inside. Kai looked around; it was a nursery, filled with cribs and other child-care products. And sitting in a rocking chair was Ramona, holding a squirming little baby.

Ramona smiled at Kai. "Hi, Papa. You want to meet your daughter?"

She held the baby out to Kai. He took her into his hands, holding her bundled body firmly but awkwardly, at a distance.

"She's not toxic," Edith said.

"She?" Kai asked, his eyes transfixed on the baby's chubby pink face. He couldn't believe this brand-new human being was his flesh and blood.

Ramona nodded.

"Does she have a name yet?" Kai asked.

Edith and Ramona looked at each other. "Not yet, just a number," Edith said. "But she's three months old now, and we probably need a name before the rest of them arrive."

Kai thought for a second, still staring at his daughter. Her cheeks were a beautiful deep red. "How about Rose?"

Ramona smiled. "Works for me."

Kai looked over at her. "So does that mean you're the mother?"

"In a sense. I gave birth to her, but we didn't use one of my eggs. Edith and I decided it was best to do this without any of the girls carrying their specific babies. We don't get to keep them, after all."

"Ramona is more than their mother," Edith interjected. "She's the brilliant mind that helped with all the engineering."

"So what's different about them, then?" Kai asked. "I mean, compared to us."

"Nothing anyone will notice at first glance," Edith said. "But believe me, they are very special. The smaller the flaws in the parents, the easier it is to craft an almost perfect human specimen."

"And what's going to happen to them?"

"That's the real question, isn't it?" Edith smiled at Kai. "It's all up to us. Little Rose here needs us to succeed."

Kai was confused. "What do you mean?"

"We can take care of these babies at the Ark for a few years, maybe, but we can't keep them hidden in the mountains forever. It's not fair to them, and there's no point. So if the world isn't ready for these extraordinary human beings right now, we have to make it ready soon enough. We need a world where the Ones, that first generation of locusts, actually have some power. Where the Ones contribute to making the rules. Where the Ones can protect the most special and vulnerable among us." Edith stared at Kai. "We're in a race against time to create that world for these babies."

Kai instinctively pulled Rose closer to his chest, already imagining everything he wanted to protect her from.

Edith reached out and slipped her finger into Rose's

tiny hand. "This right here, Kai. This is why we have to fight."

As much as he hated being manipulated, Kai knew that Edith's stunt had worked. Meeting his daughter had instantly reinvigorated him to destroy the Equality Movement. That was always what he had set out to do, and now he could see how doubly important it was. Kai wanted to make sure Rose would never be threatened with discrimination, imprisonment, the Vaccine. To ensure that, they had to deal with the problem now.

The Ones had to win.

And then there was something much more specific. Besides wanting to create a world where this tiny human being could thrive, Kai felt the weight of deep paternal instinct descend upon him. He had spent so much time reflecting on what his parents and surrogate parents had done wrong—now he had a chance and a responsibility to live up to his own standards.

After holding Rose for one more minute, Kai knew it was time to let her rest. He handed her back to Ramona and left the secluded cabin. As he walked back to his bunkhouse, Kai was certain of one thing: He wasn't going to let his daughter down.

=

The next morning Kai joined the rest of the Ones on their march to the mess hall for breakfast. Taryn fell in beside him, and Kai thought he could still sense her anger from the day before. She hadn't been very pleased about Cody making off with Agent Norton. Surprisingly, though, Taryn didn't snap at him.

"I heard the news," she said. "Where's my cigar?"

Kai smiled, relieved. "It's pretty cool, I guess. Classic Edith—always a few moves ahead of everyone else. I just can't believe she pulled this whole thing off."

"Yeah, hopefully."

"What does that mean?" Kai asked.

"Just that we have a lot more work to do if all the babies we make up here are going to be safe. We really have to get serious."

Kai felt like that was a dig at him. But before he could defend himself, Taryn walked ahead of him into the mess hall.

A few minutes later, Kai had decided to bring his food outside when he saw Taryn sitting with Cooper on the stumps.

As Kai approached, they were in midconversation.

"What about that one?" Cooper said to Taryn.

She shook her head. "Too old. We need someone who still looks like a kid."

Kai followed their gaze to a group of Ones who had been rescued from the internment camp. Construction at the Ark hadn't kept pace with all the newcomers, and now many people were eating their meals on the ground outside the mess hall.

Cooper pointed at another kid. "Okay. Him, then."

Taryn nodded. "Could work. Those chubby cheeks will help."

"The only One with baby fat, I love it," Cooper said.

Taryn shouted over to the kid. "Hey, you, come here."

A surprised ten-year-old shuffled over to Taryn.

"What's your name?"

"Henry," he said.

"And where are you from?" Taryn asked.

"Oakland."

"Oakland. Nice." Taryn nodded to herself. "You like it here at the Ark, Henry?"

"Yeah. Much better than the camp we were at. Thanks for bringing us here."

Taryn turned to Cooper, impressed. "Polite, respectful, look at that." She turned back to Henry. "Well, we're glad we got you out of there. And when the time is right, maybe you can help some other Ones, too."

She gestured that he could go back to his breakfast, and Henry walked away, confused.

"Cute kid," Taryn said.

Standing behind her, Kai couldn't believe what he was hearing. "Taryn, you can't be serious."

She responded without even turning to look at him. "You said you didn't want to be involved."

"But you're not actually going to pick one of *these* kids?"

"A scared One who escaped from a camp just trying to

make his way home? And then he gets savagely attacked by some thugs from the Equality Movement as retribution for Agent Norton's disappearance? It's perfect."

"You two are sick," Kai said.

"What about Edith? It was her idea." Taryn paused. "I thought you were on board with her vision?"

Kai knew he was trapped. Creating and protecting the next generation of Ones was admirable; killing one who already existed wasn't. He realized he was on board with some of Edith's vision, but not all of it, and that wasn't an acceptable position to have here at the Ark. The Weathermen, he knew, were about being all-in or not in at all.

"So which is it, Kai? Are you still on board with us or not?" Taryn asked.

Kai couldn't deny the creeping sensation that had finally taken hold within his gut: He was officially uncomfortable with the tactics of the New Weathermen. Even with that sinking feeling, though, he couldn't help but think of Rose. The clock was ticking on changing the world for her. She needed a society where she would be safe, and Kai had to ensure that by any means necessary.

He stared squarely at Taryn.

"I'm on board."

CHAPTER 13

CODY AND NORTON had escaped from the lake without being stopped. The next leap of faith for Cody was letting Norton make the necessary phone calls. Cody drove around for a while looking for a gas station. When she finally spotted one, she pulled around back and helped Norton over to its old pay phone.

It took Norton a minute to finally get someone on the line who understood what she was saying and believed it was her. Cody stood right next to her, listening to Norton give a series of detailed instructions: Call off the search parties, get James out of custody and onto a helicopter, meet her and Cody for the exchange—but where exactly?

Norton was looking over to Cody as if she would have some prearranged spot for the swap. But Cody had no idea what to tell her.

"Wherever we can make this happen as fast as possible," Cody said.

The colleagues coordinating on Norton's end rushed to figure it out and picked a closed-down airfield outside of Pecos, Texas. There was plenty of room for the helicopter to land and good sight lines to prevent a trap, and Cody could drive there in a couple of hours. Cody knew the government agents didn't have to worry, but she was wary for herself; she knew all too well she was doing this as a lone renegade. Worrying about that, though, seemed easier than accepting what all the logistics here meant: James was really alive, he was being tortured, and Cody had failed to rescue him—had given up on him. Or, even worse, Agent Norton and her team were lying, and Cody was about to relive his death all over again.

Norton ended the call, and Cody guided her back to the car. She jumped in and pointed it north onto a lonely, endless highway. With a long ride ahead of them, the urgency of their awkward alliance had worn off. Now it was just uncomfortable, and they both stared straight ahead.

After several minutes of silence, Norton finally spoke. "For the record, I just want to say, I'm sorry that I hurt you."

Cody, caught off guard, glanced over. "Are you really going to bring that up right now?"

"Why not? We're two people on a long car ride; we can have a conversation," Norton said. "Professionally speaking,

I still believe what happened to you was legal and appropriate considering the circumstances, but on a personal level, I'm sorry."

Some apology, Cody thought. "But you'd do it all over again, right? And you're doing similar things right now?"

Norton didn't answer.

"It doesn't make you some noble hero to acknowledge it's wrong and then continue doing it," Cody said.

"I didn't say it was wrong. Just that I wish it didn't have to happen."

"What the hell does that mean?" Cody snarled.

"Look, Cody, I don't hate the Ones. I have no desire to make them miserable. But I do have a strong desire to protect and serve my country. That's why I joined the FBI. And you have to admit, this country is on the brink of tearing apart."

"Yeah, because of the Equality Movement."

"The Equality Movement has a valid point. I don't condone their methods of enforcing it, but you understand where they're coming from, right?"

Of course Cody understood, but that didn't make it okay. She'd been having this debate for years now, and she was sick of it. No one likes competing with a genetically superior generation, but that was the price of progress. Genetic engineering could do an incredible amount of good in the world. It could ease the suffering of an untold number of people. But before all those benefits could be enjoyed, it needed to be tested, studied, tried in small doses. That's what the NIH was attempting to do. She hated people who were so shortsighted they couldn't handle growing pains on the way to something important. Something world changing.

"You really think getting rid of all the Ones is the solution?" Cody asked.

"I think this generation of Ones was a mistake, and now it's too late to fix it easily. If the Supreme Court didn't ban the technology and we continued down this path, it's clear what would happen."

"Progress?"

Norton shook her head. "No. A super race of elites who control all sectors of society. It would be inevitable. And it would be tragic."

"The Supreme Court can't stop genetic engineering," Cody said. "That's not how technology works. Somewhere, somehow, people are going to keep pushing it forward. Why not deal with it now?"

"We're not ready. Isn't that clear? I wish we were, but too many people are afraid. So for now, let's try to survive without destroying our country. That's why I want to stop the New Weathermen."

"And the rest of the Ones? The vast majority who are minding their own business and not even trying to fight back?"

"Unfortunate victims through no fault of their own.

But it's better to deal with this mistake now while we still have a chance to manage it. The sooner, the better."

"The better for who? Not for us," Cody said witheringly.

"Cody, you're not a One. You chose to put yourself on this battlefield; no one forced you."

Cody almost ripped off the steering wheel in frustration. Yes, Norton was technically correct, but Cody was tired of people trying to define her by how her stupid DNA got spliced together. Wasn't it enough just to say that every person, no matter how they were born, deserved basic human rights and dignity?

"So it's *my* fault you tortured me?" Cody asked.

"It's no one's fault—that's my point. No individual made this problem, but we can all work to solve it. That's what I'm trying to do. What about you?"

Cody shook her head. "I remember what you were like the first time we were together. You weren't just doing a job. You actually liked it. The pain, the suffering, the fear— you *enjoyed* making it happen."

"I'm glad you believed that. The more it seemed that way, the more scared you would be. But it was just an act, Cody, I promise. I'm not a sociopath."

It was almost too sad to not believe her—it meant that people could actually be that poisoned inside. Cody would never forgive Norton for her experience in captivity, but it was a relief, however small, to think that maybe Norton's heart wasn't truly in it.

"Speaking of sociopaths," Norton said, "I really need to warn you about Edith Vale."

Cody sighed. "Save your breath."

"You can still help us stop her. It's not too late. I know you can tell me where she's going right now. I know you can tell me about the Ark. No pressure this time," Norton said, making a tasteless joke, "but would you consider that?"

"I might not like Edith," Cody said, "but I would never betray the Ones. You should know that already."

Norton's tone turned even more serious. "You can't trust her, Cody. She's a maniac. And I'm sure whatever she's told you about her plans . . . there's a darker side that you wouldn't agree with."

"How would you know what she's planning? Or what I agree with?" Cody asked. "Maybe you should just stop talking."

"My job is to know. Just because we can't pinpoint exactly where she is doesn't mean we haven't been keeping tabs on her. In fact, we know a lot about her. And I can promise you, she's a self-consumed manipulator and a liar."

Cody glanced at Norton, her interest piqued.

"Still want me to shut up?"

Cody sighed. "Fine. You want to prove she's a lying nutjob, go ahead and prove it, I don't care."

"Well, for starters, she's actually Kai's mother."

Cody nearly drove straight off the road.

Edith Vale was Kai's mother?

She couldn't believe it. As she tried to count all the ways it didn't make sense, Cody realized instead it was all too perfect. Kai didn't know the identity of his parents. Edith had specifically sought him out to help with her cause. And she certainly gave him special attention. But why, then, had she abandoned him in the first place? Cody couldn't answer that, but the more she thought about Edith, the more it seemed to fit her calculating personality. She had cast Kai out on his own until he could be of use to her.

"If she's willing to lie like that to her own son, imagine what she's not telling you," Norton said.

Cody was still in shock over the revelation. "How do you even know that?"

"The database for the Ones at the NIH. They have all the birth records. There's a reason Edith didn't release everything on the List."

Cody was speechless. Norton was making enough sense that she actually believed her. She tried to figure out how Kai would take this news. Or if she should even tell him. Honestly, it was too much to deal with right now. She had to focus on getting James back first. For the time being, she just tried to drive.

Norton, however, had one final thing to say. "She'd make some mother-in-law, huh?"

Cody jerked her head to look at Norton, instantly uncomfortable.

"Don't worry, I'm just teasing," Norton said with smile. "And of course I would never say anything to James."

Cody could feel her face darkening with anger and embarrassment. She had no idea if Norton actually knew anything about her and Kai, but Cody realized her reaction had given it away all the same.

=

At the end of a couple hours of driving, Cody parked on the edge of the lone runway at the deserted Pecos airfield. They got out of the car and looked around. The only sign of movement was the tumbleweeds skipping along the cracked asphalt. A strong wind blew the heat into their faces.

After they had been waiting for a while, Norton suddenly pointed into the sky. Cody squinted and made out a dark speck moving under the sparse clouds, getting closer and closer. Eventually the rhythmic whooshing of rotors reached her ears and she saw a black helicopter dip toward the runway. Cody reached into her pocket and gripped her knife. She hoped she wouldn't have to use it.

The chopper kicked up dust as it nestled down gently, fifty yards away from their car. Someone stepped out and pulled another figure along behind him, this one with a hood over his head. They stood still next to the helicopter. Even with the distance and the dusty haze and the hood, Cody could tell it was James.

He really was alive.

Cody gasped, her legs going weak at the shock of this unlikely resurrection. She had hoped it was true; she had sensed it was possible; but not until this moment did she finally allow herself to fully believe it. James was right in front of her. Now she just had to get him.

"Tell them to send him over here," Cody said to Norton.

Norton shouted toward the chopper, but it was clear no one over there could hear her.

"They'll never give him up first without you setting me free," Norton said.

Cody was frustrated. She didn't know the rules for how to pull off a formal hostage exchange.

"Let me go halfway by myself. I'll stop and make it clear they should release James," Norton suggested.

"How do I know you won't just walk straight over and keep him?"

"I could do that right now, couldn't I?"

Cody knew this was true. She'd failed to grab a gun at the cabin, and now there wasn't much to stop Norton from making a break for it.

"You're just going to have to trust me, Cody. It's worked out well enough so far; let's keep it going."

Something about Norton's tone helped set Cody's mind at ease. Of course, all common sense dictated that Norton and the other Equality agents would screw her over. But

Cody believed Norton was truly grateful for escaping with her life intact. She knew the bullet she'd dodged by getting away from Edith, and she owed it all to Cody. Her word might actually mean something now. She hadn't been lying about James, at least.

Cody nodded. She was ready to let Norton walk out there.

Norton nodded back, took a few steps toward the chopper, then stopped and turned to face Cody.

"You're smart and talented, Cody. I was serious when I asked earlier—what are you doing to help solve this problem?" Norton reached into her pants pocket and took out a business card. "Think about it. And if you figure out a solution, let me know."

She extended the card toward Cody, who made no move to accept it. Eventually Norton shoved it into a pocket on the outside of Cody's coat. Then, with a quick turn, she walked away briskly across the tarmac. Cody watched her like a hawk, willing her to stop at the midpoint like she'd promised.

But Norton kept going, getting closer and closer to her rescue team. Cody's lip quivered in fear. She was going to lose Norton, for nothing.

Then, finally, Norton stopped.

She stood still on the tarmac and waved over to the other agent. The meaning was clear enough. He took the hood off James and pushed him forward.

James was totally disoriented, of course, and he stumbled for a few steps in the bright sunlight. Cody watched him get his bearings and lock in on her across the airfield. He passed by Norton with a look but no words. Soon he was only steps away from Cody and finally saw her clearly.

James ran the rest of the way.

When at last he reached her, Cody leaped into his arms and he spun her more wildly than the blades of the chopper. Around and around they went, squealing with ecstatic laughter and gripping each other tighter to keep from falling—and maybe even to confirm the other person was actually real.

As the helicopter with the agents took off behind them, Cody and James collapsed breathlessly on the ground in a tight embrace. Before he could speak, James began to sob. Cody held on to him, his shoulders heaving as he crumpled into her.

"It's okay, James, I'm here. You're okay now."

James kept crying.

"I've got you, baby. You don't have to be afraid anymore. I know what it's like. . . . It's all over now; you're safe."

James finally managed to compose himself. He looked into Cody's eyes, the devastation spreading across his face.

"They gave me the Vaccine."

＝

Cody drove with James away from the airfield with no destination in mind. She thought back to her experience getting picked up by James's father from her own detention. If James was anything like her, he was starving.

Spotting a billboard advertising the best barbecue in West Texas, Cody pointed them straight there. In the meantime, she told James everything that had happened since they last saw each other across the river in the Shasta woods. James listened in stunned silence—especially to the part about his brother switching sides to help him. And he didn't seem ready to talk about what he'd been through.

Luckily, Mitt's Pit, a splintery wooden building off a dusty country road, wasn't too far. Cody pulled into the lot, and they walked inside and grabbed a table. Her instincts were spot-on, because James proceeded to order half the menu. When the waitress walked away, she reached for his hands.

"All right," she said. "Tell me what happened."

James cast his eyes down. Cody remembered her reemergence into the normal world and knew it was hard. Weeks and weeks living in fear and isolation had definitely messed with her mind. Still, she was dying to know exactly what James had endured in the camp. But she could see he was completely wiped out.

At least that's what Cody hoped was going on—that James was just too tired to talk, too traumatized at the moment. She hesitated to even think about the other explanation. But of course it had occurred to her—that maybe James wasn't the same anymore.

She didn't understand yet exactly what getting the Vaccine would do to someone. Cody knew it was designed to level the playing field, so to speak, to take the small advantages possessed by Ones and mitigate them somehow. How that worked in practical terms, Cody wasn't sure. Outwardly, she couldn't see anything different about James other than his haunted expression. But maybe there was something else missing . . . a certain spark that made James *James*. She couldn't tell.

If it was actually true that he was somehow different, Cody would be devastated. First and foremost for James, of course, but also for her. She wondered if she could still love James if he was truly a different person now. And could he still love her? She remembered thinking at the river that she would love him no matter what happened, and she had meant it. But the unknown implications of his getting the Vaccine were starting to scare her.

A shiver shot down her spine as she suddenly thought of Kai. Here she was, wondering if she would always love James, when just the night before she had kissed Kai. And not just kissed him, but ecstatically imagined doing a lot more with him. Cody's heart had been crushed by the news of James's death, and then it had started to reawaken with Kai. Cody didn't plan for it to happen like that, but it did.

Could she really sit here and honestly say that she loved James after what she had done—and felt—with Kai?

Cody stared uncomfortably at James, trying to answer this question. Thankfully their food arrived, and they were suddenly up to their necks in ribs and brisket and corn bread. James dug in with abandon. After a few plates were cleaned, he seemed a little more energized.

"Look," he said, staring at Cody. "There's a lot of stuff I want to try and explain to you. I think I need a little time, though. But for now, I just want to say . . . thank you. And I love you."

Cody teared up. She didn't know how to answer. Luckily James seemed to think she was simply overcome with emotion. He stepped around the table to hold her.

"I know we've been through a lot," he said. "We'll figure it out somehow."

Cody leaned into him, truly appreciating his embrace— but also grateful she wasn't being put on the spot.

James finally stopped holding her and surveyed the table; somehow the food was almost all finished. "Should we get out of here?"

Another rock sank in Cody's stomach. "James, where will we even go?"

She saw it dawn on him that their lives had truly changed. They had no home.

"Good point," he finally said, with a sad laugh. "Not Shasta, I guess. I don't know, really. All I know is that I want to liberate the rest of the camps. And I want to find Michael."

Cody knew there was only one place where that was possible—but it wasn't exactly a place she wanted to go to. She doubted they would be welcome there.

James saw it on her face. "Where is he, Cody?"

She hesitated for a moment, but she had too much respect for James to sugarcoat it. "At the Ark, I'm sure. They're probably treating him like a prisoner. He had nothing to do with me trading Norton for you, but they might not believe him."

"That settles it," James said. "We need to go help him."

"James, that's not a good idea," she said, already imagining the anger that would await her at the Ark.

"I have to. Michael was obviously trying to make things right between us. Now it's my turn."

Cody shook her head, but she could see there was no dissuading James. And even if she knew they wouldn't be welcomed by Edith, Cody couldn't help but think about Kai and his promise that the Weathermen were ensuring a future for the Ones there. She desperately wanted to know what he meant. And at the very least, after running out on him, she owed Kai an explanation.

"All right," she finally said. "The Ark it is."

=

After their long drive and then a hike into the mountains, it was late at night when Cody and James arrived at the

Ark. Cody emerged from the trees cautiously, knowing that whoever saw her first might not be that friendly. No one was out and about, though, and Cody led James over to the woodshed where she and Michael had been locked away a few days earlier. She figured that was the most logical place to look for him, but they arrived to find the makeshift prison unguarded and empty. Michael had to be somewhere else.

They moved along the edge of the compound, with Cody fully aware she couldn't risk running into Edith. She remembered the last time she came back, when Edith had tried to strangle her. For all she knew, Edith might shoot her on sight. But maybe if they could connect with Kai, he would help them. She veered off toward his bunkhouse.

Cody realized she also had to prepare herself for the uncomfortable scenario of being in the same room as Kai and James. Should she let James know about what had happened? Not this second, obviously. And should she tell Kai about the secret that Norton had revealed? That was more complicated. But the more Cody thought about it, the more she felt that Kai deserved to know, no matter what else was going on. Maybe revealing it would even help protect her and James from Edith.

This was all weighing on her as they made their way to the bunkhouse and slipped inside. Immediately Cody ran into Taryn, staring up at them from her bed.

"What the . . . ," Taryn said.

Cooper and Gabriel were the only other people in the bunkhouse. Cody's stomach sank as she saw no sign of Kai.

Cooper sat up on his bed. "Am I crazy, or didn't this already happen?"

Gabriel eyeballed them. "I think that was a different brother?"

"I'm getting Edith," Taryn said, hopping to her feet. She turned to Gabriel and Cooper. "Don't let them leave."

"Taryn, wait," Cody said. "No Edith, please. He just wants to see his brother."

Taryn stopped and fully regarded James for the first time. "You're not . . . dead?"

"I guess not," he said, smiling at Taryn. "Pretty impressive, huh?"

Taryn was in no mood to joke, though. She turned back to Cody. "Where's Norton?"

"I had to trade her to get James."

A wave of disgust washed over Taryn's face. "And what else did you get for her? Seriously, please tell me there's more to this deal. Is the Equality Act repealed? Are the camps closed? Do we get ten prisoners to be named later?" Taryn paused. When Cody said nothing, she snarled, "Goddamn, are you stupid. Edith is going to slit your throat. Do you want a head start or not?"

"We just want Michael," James said. "Is he here?"

No one in the bunkhouse answered.

"Taryn," Cody said forcefully, "where's Michael? Didn't he come back with you guys?"

Taryn shook her head.

"So where'd he go?" Cody asked.

"To a nice big farm in the country, if you know what I mean," Taryn said coldly.

Cody glanced at James. His cautious optimism had turned to confusion.

"Seriously, Taryn, what happened?" Cody said.

"Ask Edith about it if you want." Taryn looked at James, her eyes betraying a trace of sympathy. "But I wouldn't bother. What's done is done."

Cody finally understood, and she saw James realizing it as well. He was never going to see Michael again, never going to thank him, never going to mend their broken relationship. It was crushing to watch him lose his brother all over again. Cody rushed to embrace him as he staggered against the wall.

"No . . . ," James gasped, shaking his head. "No!"

"I'm so sorry," Cody whispered in his ear as she tried to hold him up.

But James couldn't even look at her, and she didn't blame him. No matter how much he yelled, he couldn't unwind reality—the brother he'd idolized his whole life was gone forever. There were no fences to mend, no reunion to anticipate. Michael was just dead.

As Cody tried to comfort James, she heard the door to the bunkhouse open and turned her head.

It was Kai. And he was holding a baby in his arms.

Kai's eyes went wide as he saw her. Cody thought she noticed him smile ever so briefly before his face turned angry. He took a step toward her, then stopped in his tracks at the sight of James in her embrace.

"James?" he said, the disappointment evident. "How is this even . . . ?"

Before Cody explained, she couldn't help but ask a question of her own. She gestured at the baby in Kai's arms. "What's that?"

Taryn quickly chimed in from across the room. "That's called a baby. Kai's baby."

Cody looked at Kai, confused and hurt for a reason she couldn't explain.

"Why do you even care?" he asked. "You made it pretty clear you wanted no part of what's going on here."

"You didn't tell me you had a baby here."

"Would that have stopped you from letting Norton go? Give me a break." Kai glared at James. "I guess this explains why you did it."

But Cody was still staring at the squirming little thing in Kai's arms. "Taryn's telling the truth? That's really your baby?"

"Remember what I told you about the barn?" Kai asked. "Here is the first achievement. I didn't know Edith had made so much progress; I only just found out. But yeah, this is my daughter, Rose. Rose of the Ark, I guess."

Kai held the baby out for Cody to hold. But Cody took a step back. She wanted nothing to do with Kai's secret barn baby. "What do you mean, you didn't know?" she asked.

"I knew that Edith had genetically engineered a new round of embryos. Better, healthier versions of the Ones here. I just didn't know that one had been born already. And that it was mine."

Cody felt a chill go down her spine. "Is this what you meant by a future for the Ones? Some secret lab where Edith gets to experiment on a generation of super babies?"

"They're not freaks, Cody," Kai said. "Just like the Ones aren't freaks. These babies are just like us, only with even fewer flaws."

James, having composed himself a little, jumped in. "I don't get it. How does this help the Ones who already exist? Cody said you guys had some secret project to save everyone. This is it?"

Kai held his hand up to James. "You can stay out of it, all right?"

Cody tried to step in between them, sensing things were about to boil over. But James slid around her, facing off with Kai.

"I just came from a camp where the rest of the Ones are getting the Vaccine!" James bellowed. "And you're up in the mountains playing God with some embryos? What the hell is the point of this?"

The yelling caused the baby to start crying. Kai stepped aside and tried to comfort her. With great care, he built up a nice spot on his bed and laid Rose down gently. Then he stormed back toward James.

"The point," Kai started, "is to help make a world where Ones don't need to worry about things like the Vaccine. Maybe we'd be closer to that if we still had Agent Norton. But you probably think you're more important than everyone else who got screwed over."

"Hey, I never asked for that trade to happen," James responded.

"But you're fine with it, right?" Kai asked. "You think you deserve it? Isn't that how it always goes for you and your family? Whatever you want, you get?"

"Kai, stop it, you're being a jerk," Cody yelled.

"Come on, Cody, this is ridiculous," Kai said. "Why don't you just tell him the truth?"

James cast his eyes toward Cody. "The truth about what?"

Cody glared at Kai, and James looked back and forth between them, trying to connect the dots. Kai waited, but Cody didn't say anything.

"Fine, I'll just say it," he hissed, staring at James. "Cody was a lot better off with you being dead. And she knows it."

Cody tried to shout out, both to chastise Kai and to

reassure James, but it was too late. She wanted to race between them, but they were moving toward each other too fast, and the look on James's face, his long-suppressed hatred for Kai finally rising fully to the surface, made it clear there was no way to stop it now. Cody could only watch helplessly as James closed his fist, raised his arm, and started swinging.

The fight was on.

CHAPTER 14

THE FIRST PUNCH James threw landed cleanly, and Kai staggered backward. He regained his balance quickly, though, then unleashed a torrent of blows of his own. Kai's first good shot almost made him smile—it was a truly amazing feeling to finally sock that spoiled prick in the face. But Kai had no time to relish it, because James shook off the punch and began charging toward him. They collided with a sickening thud, two young men in the prime of their fighting lives, using every muscle fiber to try to hurt each other.

James's headlong rush allowed him to wrap his arms around Kai's midsection. Kai tried to twist and flip him over, but they both crashed to the floor. Forced onto his back, Kai found himself staring up at James, who started raining blows down onto him. Kai tried to slide away, but James was too strong.

Kai knew he had to eat a few punches. He covered his head and waited for an opening. In the meantime, wild shots from James bombarded his upper body.

Finally, James paused for the briefest moment and Kai pounced. From his prone position, he put all his strength into a straight right hand to James's chin. Kai knew immediately that he had tagged him on the button, and he could see James's head bobble drunkenly. Kai took the opportunity to flip on top of James, pinning him against the floor. Now this was what Kai had hoped for.

He held James down and threw punch after punch. James tried to block them, but Kai was relentless. Even in the mayhem, Kai reminded himself that this kid had known about the Vaccine and kept that secret to himself. He didn't deserve Kai's sympathy.

And most of all, he didn't deserve Cody.

This is what really fueled Kai's anger. He kept punching James to prove something to Cody. To prove that James was weak. To prove that he was superior.

As Kai raised his fist for one final, brutal blow, he looked down at James, bloodied and battered now. He was barely protecting himself anymore. With this last punch, Kai could end their fight for good.

But Kai paused, his arm cocked. He had been so

engrossed in the fight he had lost track of what was going on around him. Now he snapped back to reality. Cody was shouting behind him. His daughter was wailing over by the bed. If he was really in this fight for Cody, he knew he couldn't deliver this final shot. He knew James was still important to her, and she would never forgive him if he went too far. Kai knew he had to stop right here.

He unclenched his fist, let go of James's collar, and rolled off him. James gasped in relief and tried to sit up, but he was too weak. Cody jumped forward to check on him, and as she knelt over James, she glanced back at Kai with a disgusted expression on her face.

"Why are you guys so fucking stupid?" Cody asked.

"Simple genetics," Taryn offered. "We still haven't been able to disarm that macho idiot gene."

Kai scrambled to his feet and went to check on Rose. She was fine, but obviously the bunkhouse wasn't a great place for a baby right now. Kai also had no interest in sticking around to have Cody keep yelling at him, so he picked up Rose and barged out into the chilly night, navigating his way back to the nursery cabin. *Some father*, he thought to himself. He'd taken custody of his child for less than an hour and already exposed her to exactly the kind of violence and conflict that had ruined his own childhood. Kai vowed to do better.

Back at the nursery, Ramona was grateful to have Rose back. She seemed to sense something crazy had just happened, but Kai didn't go into the details. He said good night and retraced his steps toward the bunkhouse. It was a beautiful night, and Kai was grateful to be outside. His adrenaline was still pulsing from the fight, sweat still pouring off him. Kai tried to wrap his mind around all the new information: Cody was back. But James was alive. It was truly a scenario he had never envisioned.

Kai was stuck between wanting to scream at Cody for her betrayal and wanting to scoop her up in his arms. If only he could do both. Instead, he traversed the pathways in the woods, lost in his own thoughts, trying to cool down.

Suddenly, someone stepped out in front of him.

"Hey." It was Cody.

She emerged from the trees and blocked Kai's path.

"We need to talk," she said.

"You're nuts, you know that? Nuts and maybe suicidal, also. Why the hell did you—"

Cody cut him off. "It's cold out here. Can we go inside?"

Kai glanced around the deserted camp. The armory building was just ahead. He gestured toward it, and they walked over together.

The building was empty and dark. They pushed inside and shut the door behind them. Kai yanked on the cord of a lightbulb, which snapped on and weakly illuminated all the storage racks of weaponry. A reminder that more than fistfights were possible here.

Kai turned to face Cody. Before he could continue venting about how she traded away Agent Norton, she was already yelling at him.

"That wasn't cool back there."

"You're damn right," Kai said. "He shouldn't be here."

"He deserved to see his brother. And he's here now. You didn't have to provoke him like that—not after what he just found out about Michael." She looked at him with utter disappointment. "What happened, Kai? How could you?"

"It wasn't me. I tried to stop it. I mean, it was just really chaotic when we found you gone that morning."

"So it's my fault?"

"Of course not. If you want to play that game, Michael set this all in motion with his decision to help the Equality Team in Shasta."

"He didn't deserve to die." Cody paused. "Just like you can't blame James for being alive. Did you really have to say that to him?"

Kai knew she had a point. He softened his tone. "I just didn't expect to see him, okay? With you, I mean."

Cody paused, and he wondered what she was thinking. Kai paced across the room, away from her. Sure, he was excited to be in a dark, confined space with her, but he was still truly angry at her. Something special had happened in that lakeside cabin, and Cody had done her best to ruin it. He didn't want to forgive her so quickly, but he knew he would.

"Is he all right?" Kai muttered, not doing a great job of trying to sound sincere.

"Yeah, he'll be fine," Cody said. "I set him up to rest in my bed."

"I don't just mean from the fight. What about the . . . ?"

"The Vaccine?"

"Yeah. Did he get it?"

"He did."

Cody made it obvious she didn't want to say any more about it. Kai was curious, but he had to respect that. And then suddenly, without meaning to, they were caught staring at each other in silence. Kai had somehow made his way back across the room; he was now close enough to touch her.

Cody broke the silence. "You're right, Kai. I never should have brought him here. I never should have come back myself."

"So why did you?" He tried to make his voice stern.

"James wanted to see his brother."

"Cody, please, be honest."

She looked at the ground. "I told you. For James's sake."

"Cody. Please," Kai said again, gentler now. "Why did *you* come back?"

Cody hesitated. Kai knew there was only one answer,

however unlikely, that he could accept, that would dissolve the mountain of anger he had built up. He dropped the facade and pleaded with his eyes for her to respond.

Finally, she cracked.

"To see you."

Kai's heart almost burst from his chest. It was the best sentence he had ever heard. He knew it was possible now, that the connection he had sensed for so long was actually real. It had drawn Cody back to him, in spite of all logic.

He vowed not to lose her again.

Kai stepped forward and leaned into Cody, dying with excitement to continue their kiss. But Cody raised an arm to his chest and stopped him.

"But this isn't what I expected to see," she said.

Kai had never felt so instantly deflated. "What do you mean?"

"I wanted to see you, Kai. I couldn't stop thinking about you—"

"Exactly. Me too."

"But I show up and Michael's dead. You have a daughter. Edith is running some kind of twisted baby breeding farm. I'm just . . . confused now."

"Cody, none of that stuff has anything to do with us." He reached out to her. "Come here. Trust me."

Cody shook her head, agitated. "Yes, it does have to do

with us. Of course it does. I need to know—do you agree with what Edith is doing here?"

Kai knew Edith's methods were a little rough around the edges. But everything she'd planned in order to help the Ones had worked out in the long run. And he appreciated that she was thinking big. Considering the stakes, that's what was required.

"Edith has a vision. Even if I disagree with how we get there, I agree with that vision."

"You're not thinking clearly anymore," Cody said. "Edith has gone too far. Can't you see that?"

"You have to trust her. I promise you, Cody—you can trust her."

Kai watched as a horrified look descended over Cody's face. Tears welled in her eyes. "Trust her? No, Kai. You *can't* trust her. Edith is your mother, and she never even told you."

Kai felt a shock travel through his body and leave him absolutely frozen. But even in his paralysis, his mind was racing at warp speed. Outrage and happiness. Shame and relief. Regret and optimism. In a single instant, Kai both understood his life for the first time and was thrown into utter confusion about it. He had to remind himself to breathe.

"I'm sorry to tell you like this, but I thought you should know," Cody said softly. "I remember what it's like not to know the truth about yourself. Even if it's hard, the truth is always better."

Kai had regained control of his body and was able to talk. "How would you even know this?"

"Norton told me. She saw the medical records. And I believe her."

For some reason, Kai believed her, too. For the briefest second, a whisper of memory called out and then disappeared just as quickly.

"Still think you can trust her?" Cody asked pointedly.

But Kai darted past Cody and burst out of the armory. He raced into the woods, oblivious to his surroundings, the magnitude of this bombshell filling him with energy that needed to release. Kai ran until he was exhausted, and then finally, gasping for breath against a tree, his mind slowed down enough for him to think.

An overwhelming feeling of pride and purpose flooded over him. If Edith was his mother, Kai finally had a place in this world. He had a family and an identity and a life story that made sense. A puzzle piece had been inserted that answered so many of Kai's questions.

But he was still in the dark about one final thing: He was desperate to know why.

He needed to ask Edith.

＝

When Edith stepped out of her cabin, just as the sun peeked over the horizon, Kai was sitting on the ground, leaning against her doorway. He stood up and offered one of the two mugs of coffee he was holding.

Edith regarded him with a curious look. She seemed to sense the weight of what he'd come to talk about.

"You better come on in, then," she said, holding the door open for him.

Kai stepped inside the austere cabin. Edith sat down on the neatly made bed and gestured for Kai to take the wooden chair.

"There's something I have to ask you," Kai started. "Do you know what it is?"

Edith shook her head coyly.

"I have a feeling you do," he said.

"Go ahead, ask me."

"I heard something," Kai continued. "And I need to know if it's true. Are you . . . are you really my—"

Before Kai could finish, Edith was already nodding, an almost melancholy smile of relief creeping across her face. Kai stopped talking and just stared at her, tears clouding his vision. But he could still see Edith stand up and open her arms to him.

"Come here. Come here and let me finally hug you," she said.

Kai stood and stepped forward almost involuntarily. Edith embraced him, and he wrapped his arms around her. As his tears fell down on her shoulder, Kai squeezed as hard as he could. For the first time in his life, he was hugging his mother. The love and the pain overwhelmed him, and he couldn't let go.

When Kai finally stepped back, Edith was still staring at him with that regretful smile. Embarrassed, Kai tried to wipe away his tears.

"But . . . why?" he asked, his voice cracking, every scar on his heart visible on his face.

Edith patted the bed next to her. "Sit down, and I will try to explain. No more lies between us now. I promise."

Kai joined her on the bed, and she turned and took his hands.

"You already know that when I was a little younger than you I found out I had been genetically engineered. At the same time, the first babies were born in the NIH program, and I knew that one day I would be called on to do something to protect these pioneers. I devoted my life to getting ready. And in the middle of all that, I found myself pregnant. So I pulled some strings and made sure you were part of the pilot program—that you would be a One. I gave birth to you, and you were the most beautiful thing I'd ever seen. And the fiercest, also. I could tell even then." Edith seemed to glow at the memory, smiling more genuinely than Kai had ever seen from her.

"So I actually lived with you when I was little?" he asked.

"For a few years. It was long enough for me to see exactly who you would become someday. You had the warrior spirit, Kai. It burned in your eyes."

"I still don't understand why—"

"I was getting serious about what it would take to lead this fight one day. I started to see the valuable role I could play if I stayed on my path. I was the first locust, and all the little ones behind were waiting, growing, getting stronger. It was up to me to orchestrate the awakening. But I knew that wasn't going to be enough. I needed a partner to help me. Someone out in the world to handle the other side of the fight. Someone tough and savvy and determined. I needed a warrior. I knew you could do it, Kai. But not if you stayed with me."

Edith, getting emotional, paused to collect herself.

"I dropped you off at a fire station when you were three years old. I knew what lay ahead for you, how hard the journey might be. But I also knew that was the only way you'd be ready for what you had to do. The hardships would shape you, teach you, strengthen you. Give you the skills you would need. And eventually, when the time was right, I would call on you to be my partner."

She reached out and took Kai's hands.

"My God, am I proud of you, Kai. You came out better than I could have ever imagined, perfect even. You are built to lead this fight. I know there must have been some dark days, but I hope you realize it was worth it." Edith cast her fiery gaze directly at him. "We're together now, and we will change the world."

Kai suddenly felt the absence of his alternate childhood

like the ghost of an amputated limb. He could see it clearly in his mind, smell it, hear it, feel it, taste it even. For three years, he'd lived the life he was supposed to have. A memory of it existed, but he just couldn't quite grab it.

He had gone on to live a different life, though. One filled with more pain and misery than any child should endure. Now he knew why, at least. He felt validated that all those ordeals had been in the service of something greater, even though he hadn't known it at the time. Because Edith was right: That struggle had made him who he was. And Edith had, in fact, found him and brought them together. Now she was proud of him, and Kai couldn't fight against that. This moment with her almost made it all worthwhile. He had a mother who actually wanted to be his parent. He could figure out how to forgive her.

Edith, her face still aglow, had more to say. "This is why I used your sample in the first test with the embryos, to make Rose. There are three generations of us now. It's amazing to see."

Kai was too overwhelmed to speak.

"Our family has a unique burden, Kai. I dealt with it, you dealt with it, and Rose might have to endure it, also. We don't always have all the answers about who we are. But that doesn't mean we don't *know* who we are. In here," she said, tapping her heart, "you've always known. There's a reason I know that's true for you—you're my son." She locked eyes with him. "Now are you ready to do this?"

Kai stared back at Edith, mesmerized by her. No one had ever understood him so perfectly. Of course he was ready—he had a family to fight for now.

But before he could answer, Edith continued. "No more lies, Kai, no more hiding. I need you ready for the real war we are fighting. And that means a lot more than just these little missions, these small steps forward, this shortsighted controversy. I need you to be ready for what's past the horizon."

"Which is . . . ?" Kai asked, nervous and excited at the same time.

Edith smiled at him chillingly. "The Ones controlling everything."

"Everything? I thought you said we just need to get our foot in the door, and then we can protect the next generation."

"Kai, think about it. We are better than everyone else. The world needs our abilities; it needs our leadership. Look how incompetent our current leaders are—they got us into this mess without any way to solve it. It's because they aren't special like we are."

Edith reached out to grab him by the shoulder. "We owe it to the rest of humanity to take total control. Once we do that, there will be no chance of discrimination against Ones—because soon enough, every single person will be genetically engineered. And what a world that will be."

Kai tried to consider this vision.

"That's the truth, Kai. That's what we're really fighting for. Ones first, and Ones last. We start by earning their sympathy. Then we grab our footholds. And finally we take control. That's what I need to know you're ready for."

She stared at him, her eyes burning with the passion of someone who is alive for one singular reason. Kai had no choice but to be swept up in it.

He nodded, and Edith brushed her hand across his cheek.

"I'm so happy you know everything now," she said.

"Me too," he said, relieved but still trying to process it all.

And then, even in this complicated and life-transforming moment, Kai remembered Cody. This was a new era of honesty with Edith, and he had to say something before she found out Cody was back. He had to protect her.

"There's something else I should tell you," Kai said.

"What is it?"

"It's more of a favor, actually. You're not going to like it, but it's important to me."

"I can't agree to it until you tell me what it is."

Kai forced himself to blurt it out. "Cody came back last night. She traded Norton for James."

He watched Edith's eyes narrow with anger.

"Kai—"

"I care about her, okay? I don't want anything to happen to her."

Edith tried unsuccessfully to temper her rage. "What is it about this girl? She has undermined us at every opportunity. She just selfishly stole our best chance of winning this fight. And now she's back with her little boyfriend? Forget about her, Kai! She's not worth it!"

"I can't," he said. "And I wouldn't ask if it wasn't important."

"Kai. How can I justify it to—"

"Justify it like this: If the past seventeen years have meant anything, I've earned this request." Kai stood up and kept his eyes locked with hers.

After an excruciating moment, Edith finally nodded up at him. Before she could change her mind, Kai turned and exited the cabin.

Morning had come to the Ark, and as Kai walked away from Edith's quarters, he tried to balance his exhilaration with the seed of doubt Cody had planted about Edith's extremism. Had she lost sight of basic human morality? Did he fully agree with her plan of total domination for the Ones? Kai couldn't answer that yet. Or maybe he just didn't want to.

Instead, with a newfound spring in his step, he decided to focus on something remarkable: For the first time in his life, it seemed like it might be possible for him to have everything he'd ever wanted.

Victory for the Ones.

A place in a family.

A chance with Cody.

It had all seemed so unlikely, but suddenly Kai had everything within his grasp. It would still be a difficult needle to thread, but damn if he wasn't going to try.

CHAPTER 15

WHEN CODY WOKE up at dawn, she was in a state of total confusion, even if a few things were blatantly clear: She was on the floor of the bunkhouse, no one else was awake, and Edith Vale had one hand over her mouth and another on her throat. Cody tried to yell, but Edith kept her tightly muzzled.

As Cody tried to process what was going on, Edith knelt down, pinned Cody's arms, and stared into her eyes. The hand around Cody's throat wasn't exactly choking her, but it wasn't comfortable, either. If Edith wanted to kill her, Cody knew she could. Instead, she began to whisper.

"How dare you steal from me and then come crawling back here," Edith hissed softly. "I'm not going to forget that."

Her panic rising, Cody tried to talk, but Edith wouldn't let her.

"I've decided to grant Kai's request to not kill you—for now. But don't push your luck. Understand?"

Cody quickly realized what Kai must have done for her; she nodded vigorously. Edith glared down at her for another moment, then let go. She quickly slipped out of the bunkhouse.

Cody scrambled to her feet and took a few giant, grateful breaths as she watched Edith walk back into the woods. She looked around the bunkhouse; no one else had seen a thing. Cody checked on James, asleep on a cot next to her. He still looked a little banged up, but remained peacefully asleep.

Cody sat next to his bed and tried to calm down after almost being snuffed out in her sleep. She had known Edith might want to kill her, but her instinct to trust Kai with her safety had been correct. Taking a moment now to consider everything else that had happened, Cody realized that was pretty much the only thing she had gotten right.

Upon her return to the Ark, Cody had expected to feel a complicated mixture of excitement and confusion on seeing Kai again—but she had never expected to find him with a baby in his arms.

On the other side of the coin, Cody had anticipated that her reunion with James would have rekindled what she had always felt for him, but she couldn't deny there was something different about him. Was it the Vaccine? Or just repercussions from the trauma he'd experienced at the camp? Reuniting first with James and then Kai had only led to more questions.

As she puzzled over this, Cody heard James rolling around. She turned to see him blinking sleep out of his eyes. His face was swollen and bruised, but Cody could still easily make out his handsome, princely features. She smiled at him; they hadn't woken up next to each other in a long time, and it really did trigger an old feeling of joy.

"Come on, I'll buy you breakfast," she said, hoping that it was safe to step outside now that Edith had made her threat.

They got out of bed and headed for the mess hall. James hadn't seen the Ark in the light of day yet, and he marveled at all the camouflaged infrastructure and connected pathways.

"Kind of a Boy Scout's dream, huh?" Cody asked.

James smiled. "Was I drooling?"

"A little. Probably just hungry."

They walked in silence for a while, but then Cody had to say something. "I'm sorry about Michael. I didn't know, obviously."

James nodded. She knew he didn't blame her, but she probably did deserve some of the responsibility. James would connect all those dots eventually. By this point, all of them, James included, deserved a share of blame for the tragedies that had stained their lives. The only thing they could do was keep moving forward.

Outside the mess hall, Cody and James joined the line of Ones snaking to get inside. Ramona was right in front, and she nodded warmly at Cody. That was a relief—at least she wasn't universally hated here. After they piled their plates with food, Cody saw Edith sitting at the large table. She was going to have to pass right by her.

Cody gave a conciliatory nod as they made eye contact. She wanted Edith to know that Cody respected her request—she wasn't here to start any more trouble. Edith simply ignored her, though, and let Cody walk past.

On her way toward the door, Cody noticed something odd about the main table. As usual, it was occupied by Edith and the more senior members of the New Weathermen—Taryn, Cooper, and their cohort. But in between them today was a young boy who Cody knew had been rescued from the camp. He was in the middle of eating the most indulgent breakfast Cody had ever seen. Blueberry pancakes, cinnamon buns, and home fries were piled in front of him as he sat in a place of honor between Edith and Taryn.

Cody turned to Ramona.

"What's that little kid doing in there?" she asked.

"Oh, that's Henry. They're trying to give him a special last day, at least."

Cody was confused. "What does that mean?"

"He's going on a mission. Actually, he's really the star of the mission. Kai didn't tell you?"

Instead of elaborating, Ramona shrugged and walked away. Cody tried to read between the lines and imagine what Edith was planning. She peered back inside the mess hall, worried at what might be in store for the young One at the table.

Cody joined James on the stumps outside, but she couldn't begin to eat. A powerful thought was overwhelming her—about Edith Vale officially going too far. Since returning to the Ark, Cody had discovered one horror after another. First there was Michael's murder, an act that was totally unjustified. Then there was the revelation about what Edith was doing with the embryos, a leap forward in genetic tinkering that Cody found disturbing. And now, what? Edith was planning to send an innocent young child on a mission? Why?

The more Cody thought about it, the more she knew it was true: Norton had been right. Edith was, in fact, a maniac.

As much as Cody really didn't want more trouble, she couldn't turn a blind eye to this, either. Growing more and more unsettled, Cody suddenly saw Kai approach the mess hall.

"I'll be back in a minute," she said to James, then walked to intercept Kai before he went inside.

"Hey," she said. "You kind of ran out midconversation last night."

Kai laughed. "Yeah, sorry I took off. It was just a pretty big shock to hear that. I had to be alone for a bit."

"Is everything okay?"

"I talked to Edith. It's true. She explained everything, and I forgave her." He reached out to subtly stroke Cody's hand. "Thank you for telling me."

Cody nodded. "I'm happy for you, Kai. But I was also serious about what I said last night—Edith has gone too far. She has to be stopped."

A pained look flashed across Kai's face.

Cody kept going. "Is she really even helping the Ones anymore? It seems like she cares more about spawning some master race that she's in charge of, no matter who gets hurt in the process."

Kai started to say something, then stopped and pulled Cody around the side of the building, out of sight from the rest of the Ones. He sighed, clearly feeling torn.

"Kai, what else did Edith tell you last night?" Cody asked.

"It's not as bad as you think, okay?"

"Not as bad? But I'm basically right, aren't I? Edith is drunk on power?"

Kai looked away from her. "She wants the Ones to take over the world."

"Kai!"

"I know that sounds crazy, but what if she's right? I mean, it doesn't have to be some violent civil war. It's just people with a little more ability taking charge of things."

"Do you even hear yourself?" Cody asked. "No single group should ever be in charge of everything. Or, sorry, how did she put it? *Take over the world.*"

Kai stared at the ground. He knew it was hard to defend.

"Do you remember when I joined up with you back in Shasta?" Cody asked. "Our goal was to stop a group of people who ruled by hatred and fear. Back then the enemy was the Equality Movement. Now Edith Vale wants to do the same thing. Are you going to help me stop her?"

"Cody, now is not the time to get in Edith's crosshairs. She's still angry at you and hates that I want you here."

"Yeah, I gathered that much," Cody said. Then she stared at him. "Answer my question. Are you going to help me stop Edith or not?"

"Forget that for a minute!" Kai yelled with a flash of anger. "That's not why you came back here, right? You said you came back—"

"I don't know why I came back anymore," Cody said. "If you can't see what we need to do, then I made a mistake."

"Cody, don't mix things up," Kai pleaded. "Remember how you felt that night by the lake."

"I can't right now. I can't even remember the person who was right there with me." Cody paused, feeling like an absolute fool. Still, she couldn't deny holding a last shred of hope for Kai. "But maybe you'll shape up and remind me of what I was so excited about."

Kai, suddenly hopeful himself, looked straight into her eyes. "And if I did? If I did remind you of that feeling?"

Cody tried to choose her words carefully, because even she didn't know what would happen.

"Then I'd be in serious trouble," she said.

=

After her talk with Kai proved to be more frustrating than clarifying, Cody knew she was overdue for a similar conversation with James. She found him back at their breakfast stumps.

"Want to take a hike?" she asked.

"Yeah. We should."

Cody could sense that James had a lot to say, too.

They left the Ark's little glen and hiked higher into the mountains. There were no trails here, so they wound their way randomly through the evergreen trees. Cody wanted to get as far from the Ark as possible; that place had become toxic.

Eventually they stumbled onto a mountain stream running downhill in a narrow rush of water. Cody hopped onto a large boulder, sat down on the edge, and dangled her legs over the stream. James joined her, and they sat staring at the water in silence for a while.

Cody didn't want to shatter the rare moment of peace,

but eventually she had to ask. "So what happened there, James?"

James cast his eyes into the distance. Then he laughed. "It's funny; I never thought I was going to end up in a camp. When I stayed behind to burn down the beaver dam, I assumed I would die there, get roasted in the forest fire right along with the people chasing us. That was the whole point. But they had a helicopter right behind them. A minute after you disappeared on the other side of the river, they threw me in the chopper and we got out just in time. I had a hood over my head, but I could feel the heat scorching us. I asked Michael what it looked like, the whole forest up on flames. He didn't answer me. He never even said anything—as if I hadn't just looked him in the eye a minute earlier. As if we weren't brothers."

James dropped a pebble into the stream and watched it twist and sink in the current.

"He really did feel bad about it, James," Cody said. "He stuck his neck out for us to get Norton."

"Yeah, after he thought I was dead," James said bitterly. "Always was hard to win an argument with him."

Cody let him sit in silence for a moment.

"What happened next . . . at the camp?" she finally asked.

"They bused us up there and took us into the barracks. They weren't being cruel or anything; they made it sound like it would be pretty chill there. And temporary—they kept saying temporary. But obviously I knew what the real story was. I tried to tell the other kids, but it was too crazy for them to believe. I got caught leading a rebellion, and they dragged me into the medical building. Eventually, I was strapped down on a gurney and some guy walked in holding a syringe. Just a normal scientist-looking guy— could have been my dad."

"But it wasn't. Your dad would never have done that to you."

"No, it wasn't my dad. But it was still my dad's vaccine."

Cody couldn't argue. James was right.

"I fought like crazy, but it was pointless," he continued. "The guy walked up to my shoulder and injected me. That's the last thing I remember before I passed out. When I woke up, I was in a windowless jail cell somewhere totally different, probably the same place they took you." James laughed again. "And I guess I was officially 'dead.' Should've figured that out on my own."

"So what does it feel like now?"

"Living with the Vaccine?"

Cody nodded.

"It's hard to explain. I do feel a little different. Diminished, somehow."

"Of course you feel out of sorts," Cody said. "I'm sure that's just temporary. You had a traumatic experience—I know everything doesn't just flip back to normal."

"It's more than that, I promise."

"What if that's just in your own head?"

"What do you mean?" James asked.

"You don't seem any different, I swear. I can't tell anything's changed. But maybe that's the whole point—it makes you believe you're an inferior version of yourself. With you especially it could work like that, knowing about it beforehand like you did. Seriously, James, what if it's only in your head?"

James couldn't look Cody in the eye. He shook his head. "No, Cody. I can feel it. I used to be special and I'm not anymore. I could live with that, except for one thing—I know I don't deserve you now."

Cody reached out to cover James's mouth, heartbroken to hear him say that. But he pulled her hand away and held on to it.

"I couldn't live with myself knowing you were settling for me, knowing that I'd be dragging you down. Forget all the bullshit about being a One or not being a One . . ." James paused, barely able to speak. "All I know is that I'm not your equal anymore."

"James, stop it!"

"No, Cody, I'm serious. I knew that I lost you the moment that needle pierced my vein."

Cody tried to pull James toward her, but he resisted. It was crazy that the moment he was trying to push her away was the moment she loved him even more. That James even thought to put her first was a reminder of how incredibly kind he was. Every day of his life he proved it to Cody all over again: He cared more about her than he cared about himself.

For Cody, that was the very definition of love. And now she needed to rise to his standard.

Cody put her arms around James's head and finally got him to look at her. "Listen to me, James. You haven't lost me. I don't care how powerful you think that shot was, I can still see who you are." She locked her gaze deep into his eyes so he'd know how much she meant it. "There are some things the Vaccine can't touch. I love you still and forever, James Livingston."

As James stared back at her through his tears, the beginning of a smile fought its way onto his face. He couldn't help himself; in spite of all the arguments he had made, Cody saw that she had actually convinced him. They both leaned forward and passionately kissed for the first time in far too long.

They had remembered that they deserved each other.

＝

They spent the rest of the afternoon lounging by the stream, and when the sun started to dip below the highest peaks, they finally got moving back to the Ark. It was a long downhill hike, and as they started walking, Cody couldn't help herself: She picked out a nice round stone and kicked it in front of James's feet. It was their old game, seeing if they could get the rock all the way down the hill. James laughed and gave it a little boot.

Now that the old James was reemerging, Cody wanted his take on what was happening at the Ark. She filled him in on everything she had learned, and he listened in quiet shock. When she was done, he just shook his head.

"You're right. Edith Vale pushing for world domination doesn't help the Ones," he said.

"Exactly."

"When you dragged me into this fight back in Shasta, what did you care about? The Equality Act. The camps. The Vaccine. The legalized persecution. All of Edith's wild violence does nothing to change that." He stopped walking and turned to Cody. "We've got to do something."

"I know. But what?" she asked.

"All I know is there are thousands of other Ones still stuck in the camps. Being lined up for the Vaccine. I know how scary that is. We have to stop that somehow."

"Edith doesn't care who gets hurt as long as she keeps consolidating power. For her, the uglier things get, the more important she seems," Cody said.

"Then forget Edith. We need to go above her."

"There is no *above* Edith. The Ark, the Weathermen, Edith—that's the whole movement."

James was lost in thought for a moment. Cody looked for their rock, but they had somehow lost track of it.

Then James smiled. "Okay, so we don't forget Edith, but we do steal one of her ideas."

Cody looked at him dubiously. "Which one?"

"Remember why she wanted to kidnap Norton? For leverage. To negotiate. To make a deal."

"And . . . ?"

"Let's play that game. Let's give up Edith to make a deal—a deal that actually does something for the Ones right now."

Cody suddenly saw what James was building toward. The other side was already fearful of Edith and her extremism, and desperate to stop her at all costs—Cody and James had both learned that all too painfully. Yet the Equality agents didn't even know half of what she was up to. The full extent of Edith's plans would chill them to their bones. But if they knew what was happening and then were given a chance to prevent it . . . that would be a serious bargaining chip. Enough, maybe, to put the Equality Act on the negotiating table.

Cody knew this would be difficult to execute. They ran the risk of betraying their cause and achieving nothing at all. It had to be handled very delicately, in secret, at the highest levels of the government. Yet Cody saw a glimmer of hope in this plan; with one deft move, she thought she just might be able to pull it off.

Cody looked at James and nodded.

Then she dug into her coat pocket, searching for a business card.

=

Cody sat alone in the booth of the diner, staring out the window and self-consciously nibbling on her slice of pie. Even though it was the middle of the night, she had never been so wired.

After getting back to the Ark with James, Cody had waited for nightfall and snuck away in the dark, hoping to avoid any suspicion. She hiked down the mountain using a flashlight, back to where she had stashed their trusty getaway car from Texas. Then she drove out of the mountains and back into normal civilization to find a phone, checking her mirrors the whole way. Cody didn't know exactly who might be following her, but if anyone was onto her plan, it would be a disaster. No one could know about this meeting.

She had made it undetected to this random roadside diner off exit sixty-eight of Interstate 5. There was hardly anyone else there, and the few other customers might as well have been asleep. Cody was the only one tapping her silverware nervously against the table.

Even as the waitress checked in with her, Cody didn't take her eyes off the diner's front door. Her anxiety at this point was kind of pointless—if Cody was about to get screwed over, it was too late to change anything.

And then, right on time, Agent Norton walked in.

She spotted Cody in the back booth and approached alone, while Cody tried to glean if anyone else there noticed her arrival. Half-asleep, all of them, still.

Norton arrived at the table and paused. "May I sit?"

Cody nodded.

Norton slid into the booth and stared at Cody. "Thank you for inviting me. What's good here?"

"Huh?"

"Food, Cody. Any recommendations?"

But Cody didn't answer. A fit man in a denim coat had just entered the diner and was walking briskly toward their table. Cody locked in on him. Only a few feet away, he reached into his coat pocket. Cody grabbed the butter knife off the table. She was not going to be taken captive again. She promised herself that would never happen. If that meant she had to defend herself with a butter knife, she was ready.

But the man took his hand out of his pocket and fumbled with some coins. He glided past the table and stopped at the pay phone behind them. Cody, however, didn't let go of the knife.

Norton watched all of this with bemusement. "You can relax, I promise. I came alone, just like you said. I traveled all night, and I'm in no mood to play games." Norton paused. "So let's get to it. Why did you ask me here?"

Cody stared at Norton, trying to determine if she was being honest. At this point, she just had to trust her. There was no backup plan after this one.

"You asked me at the airport what I was doing to solve the problem of the Ones," Cody said, trying to speak as directly as possible. "I'm ready to get serious about it. But I need to know if you are, too."

"You know I want to find a solution."

"Do you want it badly enough to suspend the Equality Act?" Cody asked pointedly.

"And what would that solve?"

"It's not what it would solve, it's what it would prevent."

Norton nodded for her to go on.

Cody leaned in closer. "What if I told you that Edith was intent on having the Ones take over our entire society? And what if I told you she had figured out a way to create the next generation of Ones, even more intensely engineered than those who already exist? And what if I told you the violence and destruction won't stop until the Ones take control and turn genetic engineering into the law of the land?"

Cody finished and stared at Norton.

"If all of that was true, I'd be very scared," Norton said. "I take it from your phone call, you are, too."

"There's a lot of stuff at the Ark I disagree with. But I also disagree with the inhumane and illegal persecution of Ones that's taking place right now."

"And you really think I can snap my fingers and change all of that?"

"You tell me. Can you?" Cody asked.

Norton thought for a second. "The Equality Task Force has the power to implement the law as we see fit. Let's say I could adjust our policies—what do you propose?"

Cody was ready with her list of demands. "You liberate the internment camps. You announce that all the Ones have been vaccinated and normalized. You declare the threat over. And you insist on the repeal of the Equality Act." Cody paused. "In return, I'll give you Edith, the Ark, and the second generation of Ones."

That was the deal. Now the two adversaries locked eyes across the table. It was almost unbearable for Cody. She felt like she was an inch away from achieving what she had always wanted—justice for the Ones. But to get it, she was going to have to commit a brutal betrayal. And that was only if Norton said yes.

Cody went for one final push. She trusted her gut, changed her tone, and spoke to Norton like a normal human being.

"It's crazy to think about, but we can end this thing right here, you and I," Cody said. "The Ones who are alive won't be punished anymore. And that tidal wave of dominance that everyone is so afraid of will be nipped in the bud. We can save this country from tearing itself apart."

Still, Norton sat in silence. Cody tried to imagine what

was going through her mind. There was a tremendous leap of faith required to agree to this deal. But maybe, with their history, they were the only two people who could pull it off. Tormentor and victim. Captive and savior. Partners who had closed a deal together once before.

"How do I know my team won't be walking into a trap?" Norton finally asked.

"You can't. How do I know you'll keep your word?"

Norton thought for a second. "You can't."

"Exactly," Cody said.

There was nothing left to negotiate now. They were both on equally precarious footing. All they had was trust, and they both knew it.

Finally, without another word, Norton extended her hand across the table. Cody reached out and shook it.

They had a deal.

CHAPTER 16

KAI PRACTICALLY CARVED a dent into his mattress with all his tossing and turning throughout the night. Cody had made it perfectly clear to him earlier that morning: She could never love him if he kept supporting what Edith was doing at the Ark. Of course Kai saw Cody's point—Edith's plan had gone from daring to dark. It had started as a fight for justice and transformed into a grab for absolute power. But it was hard for Kai to disavow Edith; she was his mother, after all, and he had just found her.

Dinner at the mess hall earlier that night had been particularly uncomfortable. Kai didn't know where Cody was, but he was grateful she wasn't there. Taryn and her crew were giving the Henry kid a last supper of sorts, as if spoiling him rotten for one full day made up for killing him. They planned on leaving the Ark with him in the morning.

Kai had watched from across the room, trying to figure out a way to stop this false flag killing. Appealing to Edith and Taryn hadn't worked. As a last resort, Kai knew he could force his way onto the mission and sabotage it from there. But that would only be a temporary reprieve—Edith's plans were too grand for him to stop alone.

Still, Kai couldn't help being tempted by how easy it would be to simply trust Edith. If he would just get on board, if he would unreservedly put Edith first, his life would be so much simpler. Granted, he wouldn't have Cody, but he reminded himself of everything else he could keep. His role in the fight against the Equality Movement. His standing at the Ark. His daughter. His mother. His entire identity, basically.

Everything except Cody.

So why wasn't he comfortable choosing that? Maybe it was because he knew every freckle on Cody's face by memory. Because he knew the three different ways she laughed. Because he could remember every brave thing she did, every brilliant remark she said, every selfless gesture she performed. In the relatively short time Kai had known her, he had come to an unwavering conclusion: She was perfect.

He could recall each moment that led him to this belief. Her beauty when he first approached her in the diner. Her courage walking into that first New Weathermen meeting. Her fear when he snuck into her bedroom in Shasta. Her poise during the school takeover. Her vulnerability when she'd returned from being captured. Her stubbornness as she'd run toward the lab bombing. And now he fully saw her passion for justice as she tried to show him where the Weathermen had lost their way. He loved all of it.

Kai almost had to laugh at the idea of Cody's perfection. That's what this whole controversy was about, after all. Scientists had figured out how to make human beings more and more perfect. Those who were left out had grown scared. And as the two sides raged over this issue, Kai had discovered someone who truly was perfect, science be damned.

All the success in the world with the other parts of his life would never make him happy. Kai finally had to accept it: Cody was more important to him than anything else. It was almost a relief to admit it to himself, and Kai suddenly felt elated. Cody had been clear about what was required for them to be together. And deep down, he knew she was right about what was going on here. He had to disavow Edith.

If that meant leaving the Ark and Rose behind, too, he could handle it. It didn't mean he had to stop fighting for the Ones, though. He and Cody would forge their own path.

Kai craved sleep now more than ever—it meant morning would come sooner. And in the morning, he'd make the craziest and best decision of his life.

He would stop the killing of an innocent child. He would defy Edith. He would choose Cody.

≈

A few hours later, Kai hopped out of bed like it was Christmas morning, or at least how he imagined kids in normal homes hopped out of bed on Christmas. He had come to a firm and beautiful decision: He was going to devote his life to reminding Cody about the feeling they had shared. Kai knew she was scared about what that would lead to. That didn't bother him, though—it was the good kind of scared. He knew he could win her over.

Cody's bed was empty—still no sign of her since yesterday morning—so Kai made his way to breakfast, hoping to find her there. A bunch of Ones were already eating; Taryn, Cooper, and some others were trying to get an early start on their mission. Neither Cody nor James was around, but Kai wasn't worried; he'd told Cody to keep a low profile for a while and hoped that she was listening to him.

Kai had just joined the breakfast line when an ear-splitting sound rang out through the woods. As everyone looked around, confused, a voice boomed from a megaphone.

"YOU ARE SURROUNDED BY MEMBERS OF THE EQUALITY TASK FORCE."

Kai couldn't believe it.

"DO NOT RESIST AND DO NOT RUN."

This was really happening.

"WE HAVE THE ENTIRE CAMP SURROUNDED."

The Ark was under attack.

"I REPEAT: FOR YOUR OWN SAFETY, DO NOT RESIST."

Kai locked eyes with Taryn. They didn't need to say anything. In an instant, they were both moving to the door.

They burst out of the mess hall and started racing across the central area of the Ark. As Kai ran, he glanced into the woods and saw Equality agents approaching through the trees.

"Stay down!" he yelled to Taryn.

They ducked their heads and tried to run faster, cutting every angle and hurdling every obstacle. Both of them knew how important it was to get to their destination. They were heading for the Armory.

Oddly, no bullets whizzed past as they ran. It seemed to Kai that the Equality Team sincerely wanted to seize the Ark peacefully. But as he and Taryn crashed through the door of the armory, Kai knew that even if that was true, it was impossible. The Ark wasn't going down without a fight.

Gabriel was already in the armory, loading weapons. He

smashed a clip into an assault rifle and threw it across the room to Kai, just as Cooper arrived next, breathing hard but joining in without pause. Everyone grabbed a gun and loaded up.

"Don't fire until we can see more of them," Kai said. "Once this starts, it's going to get real ugly, real fast."

"How the hell did they find us?!" Taryn shouted in frustration.

Kai shrugged. He didn't know, either.

"There's no way we make it out of here," Gabriel said calmly.

"Yes, there is!" Kai yelled. "We know these woods. We have plenty of ammo. We are going to get out there and be smart and fast and pick them off one by one. And I can promise you this: I am not surrendering to get dragged away to some camp."

As the other Ones nodded, Edith burst into the armory. She immediately loaded herself up with weapons.

"They're everywhere—we need to get moving," she said. "Find a way to get to the barn; we'll make our stand there. We need to protect the barn at all costs."

Edith turned to Kai. She reached out and touched his cheek. "Be careful out there."

Just that morning Kai had resolved to pick Cody over her. But that wasn't going to stop him from fighting like hell by Edith's side. His decision had been made before the

Ark was under attack. Their enemies were coming after them now, and Kai had no doubt that he and Edith were on the same team.

He nodded back at her. "You too."

Edith turned and ran out of the armory. Kai heard her gun open up, and suddenly there was gunfire roaring back from the trees. Cooper and Gabriel followed her. Kai slipped his head out, looking for an opening. Before he ran, he turned back to Taryn. They weren't on the best of terms currently, but Kai knew their bond ran deeper than that.

"One last mission for old time's sake?" he asked.

"Let's do it."

Kai held her gaze. "I wouldn't want to run out there with anyone else."

Taryn stared back at him. She understood what he meant. "Then get going, why don't ya?" she said with all the irritation she could muster.

Kai smiled and darted out of the armory.

The pathways of the Ark had become a circular shooting gallery. Bullets flew in every direction as Kai dodged from one place of concealment to the next. At various points he caught sight of an Equality agent in the woods and sprayed the area. But mostly, he tried to navigate to the barn.

When he finally made it there, he saw some of the other Ones had taken cover behind trees at the front entrance.

Kai sprinted over and slid in behind them. The Equality Team hadn't reached this area of the Ark yet, but Kai knew it was just a matter of time.

He turned to look at the barn. Dozens of fertilized embryos sat in there, ready to one day come to life as the most genetically engineered babies ever born. The potential inside that building was amazing. It was worth fighting for.

And somewhere deeper in the woods, Kai assumed Rose was sleeping in the nursery cabin. If he made it away from the barn alive, he'd be racing over there next.

A volley of bullets sliced past them and smacked into the barn. Kai pressed himself to the ground and angled his body around the tree. Agents were marching forward through the woods. Kai took aim and started firing.

The Ones had a pretty good defensive position, and they managed to slow the Equality Team's advance. But Kai knew they couldn't hold this spot forever. Eventually the agents would encircle them and start to tighten the noose.

"Hey," Kai called out to Taryn, a few feet away behind a different tree.

He gestured that he was going to track back into the woods and try to outflank the approaching agents. If the Ones stood any chance, they needed to play a little offense. Taryn understood his hand signals and nodded.

Kai ran around the side of the barn and slipped into the

woods. He gave himself a wide angle and circled back to where the Equality Team was hunkered down. Every sense was locked in for Kai, who was instantly and easily in his element now. He moved carefully but quickly, preserving the element of surprise.

After a few minutes, Kai saw he was approaching the agents from the side. But they had moved closer and closer to the barn. Less gunfire came from the Ones' direction, and Kai wondered how many people were still left fighting.

As Kai crept forward, almost ready to spring his ambush, he saw some of the agents make it all the way to the edge of the barn. The Ones who'd been making their stand there had either all fled or been shot. Still, Kai rose from his crouch to fire from the agents' blind side. He had the perfect window to attack.

Raising his gun to take aim, Kai heard the bullet before he felt it.

The concussive pop was close to him, but it hadn't come from his gun. And then, only an instant later, he felt the hot pain of the bullet tear through his rib cage, explode in his chest cavity, and knock him to the ground.

Suddenly there was an Equality agent standing over him, gun pointed at Kai's face. The agent looked tense and nervous, his gun shaking as he tried to keep it level. Kai closed his eyes, waiting for the final shot.

It didn't come.

"Got one down over here!" the agent yelled, then he kicked Kai's gun away and picked it up.

Kai lay motionless on the ground, confusion overwhelming him. He wanted to stand and fight, but his body wasn't listening. A tremendous weight was bearing down on his torso, and he could hear his heartbeat pounding in his head. Finally Kai had the courage to touch his hand down to his chest. He lifted it back up, totally covered in blood.

There was no way to sugarcoat it—he was dying.

Kai craned his neck to look over at the barn. He saw the Equality Team walking around comfortably now. They were putting Gabriel in handcuffs. They were prodding Cooper's lifeless body. Every other One he saw was sitting on the ground in a line, captured. The shouts and gunshots around the Ark had completely subsided now, and Kai knew the Ones had been vanquished. Despite his mixed feelings about her plans, Kai's heart still broke for Edith, wherever she was right now. The Locust Project she had worked on for so many years was in shambles. The swarm had been thwarted. Her dream was dead.

Then Kai had a depressing thought. Maybe this was inevitable for Edith's locusts. They wait patiently for years and then swarm in a magnificent wave of destruction. But eventually, and all too quickly, the whole swarm dies together.

Kai's thoughts were interrupted by a rustling in the

woods behind him. He shifted his head to follow the sound. Sure enough, there was Taryn, thirty feet away, staring back at him.

Of course Taryn hadn't succumbed yet. She never would be taken alive, Kai knew. That's what he always loved about her. And now he hated that she had to see him dying like this. Kai stared back at her, and before he could even share a moment of commiseration, she was gone, disappearing silently into the woods. Kai knew she would make it.

There was nothing more he could do, so Kai looked to the sky, a beautiful crystalline blue on this fresh alpine morning, and he resolved to spend his last few moments alive enjoying this final glimpse of natural beauty.

As Kai lay alone now, some activity at the barn caught his attention. He lifted his head to look, and even though he didn't want to believe it, what he saw suddenly explained everything. Agent Norton was walking up to the barn.

And walking calmly at her side was Cody.

Kai winced with a pain far greater than the burning in his chest.

It was Cody who had given up the Ark.

It was Cody who had betrayed them.

Only an hour earlier Kai had sprung out of bed desperate to find her and tell her that he'd do whatever it took to be with her. Now he finally had his eyes on her, and everything he'd wanted to say was pointless. Cody had asked him to choose between her and his cause. Kai had never thought to ask the same of her. Regardless, she had made her choice very clear.

Kai only hoped that Cody had made sure this was worth it. He could never forgive her this betrayal, but he knew Cody was smart. Maybe, just maybe, she had struck some kind of deal that could justify what was happening right now. Even in his agony and horror, Kai realized that Edith's prescient words had come true—if you scare the other side badly enough with your extremists, they might just make a deal with the moderates. It seemed that everyone had played their part perfectly. Maybe crazy Edith had saved the Ones, after all.

As Cody wandered with Norton through the battlefield in front of the barn, he saw her start looking around the adjoining woods. A moment later, an Equality agent pointed in Kai's direction. Cody turned and saw him from afar.

With deep shame, Kai felt his heart surge. Even knowing full well the treachery she had just pulled, Kai was still desperate to share one last moment with her. He lay as still as possible while she approached, willing his body to stay alive for just another minute longer. At last, she reached him and knelt beside him.

Kai looked up and saw tears in her eyes. She could see his bullet wound and knew just as well as he did what it meant.

"Kai . . . I'm sorry," she said. "No one was supposed to get hurt."

Even dying, Kai had to laugh. Cody knew the Ones at the Ark would never surrender without a fight; of course people were going to get hurt. But there was no point and no time to argue with her. He had more important things to say.

"I was looking for you earlier. I couldn't find you," he said. He paused, taking a painful breath. "There was something I wanted to tell you."

Cody took his hand between hers and nodded.

Kai looked up at her, ready to reveal his decision. He wanted Cody to know that on the last day of his life, he had picked her over everything else. At the end, she was what mattered most, and for him to be sure of that for even a single day had been a beautiful gift. Kai gathered the strength to tell her and opened his mouth to pour his heart out.

And then he stopped.

Cody had seen him readying to speak; she leaned in closer to him.

But Kai had gone silent.

"Kai, what is it?" Cody asked. "You can tell me."

Kai stared up at her, the tears building in his eyes now.

"Kai, talk to me. I'm so sorry. I did it for all the other Ones." She paused and waited for him to speak. "Please, talk to me."

Kai knew exactly what he wanted to say.

And he knew, for her sake, he shouldn't say it.

No good could ever come from the speech that Kai wanted to deliver. No joy, no meaning, no solace would be gained from telling Cody how much he loved her. It would only be selfish. Kai was about to die, and dead guys couldn't be happy.

Cody, on the other hand, had a life to live. She had a future that Kai wasn't a part of. Maybe her future was with James. Maybe it was with someone else, or no one at all. But Kai had to let her go into that future without him. He closed his eyes and tried to imagine how happy she might be. That was enough. For now, it would have to be enough.

Looking up at Cody, Kai caught the words in his throat and sealed them away forever.

Cody still stared down at him, her hand reaching out to touch his face. The reality of their world was spinning in chaos and streaked with blood, but their little patch of forest was filled with peace and perhaps, Kai hoped, even love. He was barely breathing now, and he could see that Cody had given up on him speaking again. So they just locked eyes and held still for a moment, the bond between them acknowledged but unsaid. As Kai fought to stay alive, Cody leaned in and gave him a gentle kiss on the cheek.

Kai closed his eyes, shutting off all his other senses to feel her lips ever so briefly one last time. He was ready now. But one last shred of his spirit still remained. With his dying breath, Kai hoped for one final act of goodness.

Turning toward Cody's ear, Kai used all his strength to whisper.

"There's a cabin, deeper in the woods, a nursery . . ."

CHAPTER 17

WHEN KAI'S VOICE trailed off and his labored breathing finally ceased, Cody closed her eyes and kept her hands pressed to his face. This was not what she had wanted to happen.

Cody's deal with Norton had been straightforward. After Cody revealed the location, Norton was going to lead the Equality forces to the Ark, where they would apprehend Edith and peacefully deal with the other Ones. Of course, Cody knew that was wishful thinking; the Ones at the Ark were wired to defend themselves, but she hoped the Equality Team could subdue them without deadly violence.

It was too much to ask, though, and now Kai was dead. A chill descended over Cody. The reality of such a vibrant life being taken away left her feeling totally empty.

There was no twisted logic that Cody could use to make herself feel better. Kai was dead because of her, and she would have to live with that guilt for the rest of her life. The only solace was that maybe his death would help achieve the results he so passionately wanted. Cody wasn't going to rest until the Ones were free. She would honor him by continuing his fight. And maybe—if it was even possible—by fulfilling his final request.

Cody thought back to all the extreme emotions she'd gone through since meeting Kai: fear, admiration, anger, disappointment . . . and at one point, maybe something approaching love. It seemed impossible to be sitting next to his dead body now. Through it all, Kai had always made her feel so alive.

As Cody considered the events of the past day, a sad sense of relief came over her. At least now she had a measure of clarity about her and Kai. He had made his decision and died defending what was most important to him. As it turned out, it wasn't Cody, it was the Ark. Cody was a little surprised by this, maybe even offended, but also grateful. She had made the right choice reconnecting with James. Kai, it was now clear, would never have been able to truly love her.

Cody sat by him for one final moment, saying good-bye, and then she stood up and walked back toward the barn.

Many of the Equality agents were milling around when

suddenly there was a big commotion just behind the building. Cody hustled over just in time to see Edith dragged out of the woods.

The agents pinned her arms and rushed her over to where Norton stood in front of the barn. They threw Edith roughly to the ground, piling on unnecessarily to handcuff her. Then they stood her back up to face Norton.

"It's good to see you again, Edith," Norton said.

Edith laughed in her face. "Congratulations on your big accomplishment. You found the Ark. As if that will do anything to—"

"We're going to stop the cycle of violence in this country. Shutting this place down is a big part of that."

"You don't get it, do you?" Edith asked.

"What's that?"

"You can't stop what's coming any more than you can stop the wind. Even if you burn this place to the ground and keep the Ones locked up forever, you'll still lose. You are fighting against the inevitable. And the inevitable always wins."

Norton didn't respond, and Cody sensed that part of her must have agreed with Edith. Maybe they were just pointlessly fighting back against something that would be too powerful to stop. But this was the world they lived in right now. There was no shame in trying to make sure it didn't spin out of control on their watch.

As Cody contemplated this, Edith noticed her for the

first time. She struggled against the agents holding her. "Of course you're behind this."

Cody stared back at her. "No, Edith, *you* are the reason this happened. You stole the Ones' cause and made it your own. You took their fight and turned it into a war."

"Easy for you to say, when you're not even a One," Edith said, scowling. "You never understood what was at stake here. You're not even a traitor. You weren't one of us to begin with."

"You're right, I'm not like you," Cody said. "I want justice, not power."

"Now you'll get neither. Just blood on your hands instead."

"I'm sorry that people died here today. It's a totally senseless tragedy. And I'm especially sorry about Kai. But that's on you, not me."

"Kai?" Edith asked. "Where is he?"

"He's dead."

Cody watched closely, expecting Edith to shatter at this news. But Edith remained composed, hardly seeming to acknowledge she had just lost her son. It was either an amazing display of self-control, or a revelation of her truly dark soul. After everything that had happened, Cody sensed it was the latter.

"He was a good soldier," Edith said. "A good soldier who made one bad choice."

Cody held Edith's gaze. "Yeah, his one mistake was following you. But you know what? I actually get it. I know that when you started out you had noble goals. And I also know how easy it is to get tempted by power and blinded by rage. I've seen it on both sides." She stole a glance at Norton. "I've even experienced that rage myself. But it doesn't accomplish anything. It only leads to more rage. Maybe, someday, you'll remember the noble goals we all started with and be part of the solution."

Edith didn't respond, only glared. Cody knew it would be a tough journey for Edith, but she hoped it might still be possible for her to rediscover her original honorable intentions. It seemed unlikely now, but as the Equality agents led her away, Cody was sure Edith would have plenty of time to think about it.

While the other agents busied themselves with breaking down the door of the barn, Cody made her way back to the main area of the Ark. All the Ones who had surrendered peacefully were being watched there by a group of tense agents.

Cody spotted James and walked toward him. They hadn't seen each other since she had departed the night before to head for the diner.

"I guess Norton took the deal?" James said.

"We've got to make sure she follows through," Cody said to him, "but I actually trust her."

"You did the right thing, Cody."

Cody thought for a moment. "I hope so."

She looked around at the Ark. The lifeless bodies of Ones and Equality agents littered the woods.

"Was it crazy here when they came through?" she asked.

"It was calm at first. But Kai, Taryn, Edith—you had to know they wouldn't go down without a fight," James said. "I did what you told me, found a hiding spot until it was safe to surrender."

Cody nodded, still feeling the powerful guilt.

James gazed toward the barn. "Any sign of . . . ?"

"They captured Edith. Not sure about Taryn. And Kai—Kai's dead."

"I'm sorry, Cody."

She appreciated the gesture. James knew that Kai meant something to her, even if he hated him. He knew that she was hurting. Cody leaned into him and they embraced. As Cody peered over his shoulder, she saw little Henry sitting on the ground. He looked up and caught her smiling at him; in his mind, probably just another example of all the weird attention he'd been getting. He had no idea that his presence was a much-needed affirmation for Cody.

Her moment with James was interrupted when Norton walked over. She pointed back to the barn.

"We got the door open. Do you want to come see?"

Cody nodded. She grabbed James, and they followed Norton to the barn.

At the entrance, Cody paused, then stepped through the steel doors for the first time. She emerged into a cavernous laboratory, with high-end equipment filling the space. Cody thought back to her old life, before the List and the torture and the bombings and all the death . . . her "childhood," she could probably call it now. Back then, all she ever wanted was to work in a place like this someday. Today, however, walking through the rows of workstations, she was appalled. Edith had been running a renegade genetic engineering lab. What she had done in here was subject to no laws or oversight, only Edith's unchecked ambition.

At the back of the barn, Cody watched as the Equality agents handled a shelf of engineered embryos. They were just tiny collections of cells, suspended in a saline solution in narrow beakers, ready to be implanted into a human womb. Norton stood supervising as each one was packed away.

Cody had seen enough. She was ready to leave the barn and the Ark for good.

She and James went back outside, and Norton joined them a minute later. "Is there anything else we should know about up here?" Norton asked.

Cody hesitated.

"Cody?"

They had a deal, Cody knew, and she wanted to behave in good faith. But she also had made a promise to Kai.

"That's everything," Cody said.

Norton breathed a sigh of relief, the weight of this ugly

fight finally showing on her. She looked at Cody with almost a hint of friendship in her eyes. "Where are you two heading from here?" she asked.

Cody looked at James. He shrugged.

"Not sure," she said.

"Well, I have some important business to get to in D.C., don't I? I'm going to hop on the helicopter right now. Do you want a lift out of the mountains?"

Cody thought for a moment, then shook her head. "No thanks. I'm kind of looking forward to the quiet hike down."

"Suit yourself." Norton formally offered her hand to Cody. "Good-bye, Cody. We'll talk soon, I'm sure."

Cody reached out and they shook hands, sharing one final look before Norton walked away. Despite their unlikely alliance, Cody sincerely hoped she would never see her again.

=

A few hours later, Cody and James were driving out of the Cascade Mountains. They had hiked down to the getaway car and pointed it south. Cody laughed when she got in the disgusting, barely functioning car. This throwaway purchase had turned out to be an unlikely hero in what had the potential to be a series of world-changing events.

As Cody drove the winding roads, she wondered if

everything that had been set in motion would, in fact, change their world. With Norton holding up her end of the bargain, she believed it would. The Ones who were alive could lead normal lives. The fearful masses in the Equality Movement could sleep easier, believing that the Vaccine had been applied. And for now, the Supreme Court wasn't allowing any more Ones. Maybe it would only last for a brief moment in time, but harmony was possible.

And Cody wasn't going to live in fear over the next crisis. A new problem would arise eventually, of course, and her town, her country, her world would once again be pushed to the edge. But Cody was comfortable with what would happen at that tense moment: A group of brave, inspired individuals would fight back. The fight might get ugly and bloody and bleak, but Cody had a new confidence that reason and justice would prevail. All it would take was a little understanding from both sides. Not the easiest thing to achieve, Cody knew, but always possible.

On a smaller scale—and driving through these mountains certainly made her feel small—Cody now understood the reservoirs of strength she was capable of tapping. It meant she didn't need to fear anything in her own life. After what she had been through, Cody knew that she had within her an answer for anything.

Already, Cody was excited for her next challenge. She

looked over at James beside her. They had a life to build together and a relationship to rebuild. Cody knew they could pull it off. They had just spent the last few months going back and forth, challenging the other to rise to a new definition of love. Each time, no matter how unlikely, they had been able to meet that new standard. Doing that forever with James sounded thrilling.

And finally, Cody knew they had to honor everyone who hadn't been as lucky as them. James's father and his brother. Kai and all the other Ones whose lives had been ruined by the Equality Movement. In Cody's mind, Kai represented everyone who had fought for the cause of justice and died. She was proud to devote herself to honoring his legacy.

She would do it by never being silent in the face of intolerance. Never hesitating to meet force with force for the right cause. Never giving up in the face of insurmountable odds.

Cody knew that was a high bar to set, and wondered if it would really be possible to keep Kai's legacy alive. But then she couldn't help smiling as she turned to look at the tiny bundle secured in the back seat.

Kai's daughter was staring back at her with red cheeks and wide eyes.

After giving Rose a little squeeze, Cody reached out for James's hand. There were three of them now, all born in vastly different ways and for vastly different reasons. They were conceived by joyous accident and by evil intent, to fill voids and to be pioneers, to change the world and to be changed by it. But Cody knew none of those differences mattered.

As they drove ahead together, they were equals.

ACKNOWLEDGMENTS

I'd like to thank all the people at Imprint who helped craft this book and transform it from pipe dream to reality. First and foremost to my editor, Erin Stein, for caring about this story as much as I did. Then to Rhoda Belleza and John Morgan, who kindly saved me from my worst impulses. And to everyone else behind the scenes—especially Nicole Otto, Brittany Pearlman, and Ashley Woodfolk—thank you for all the hard work in helping me create this series.